LOUISIANA BOUND

DONNA HANKINS

Donna Hankins

ISBN: 978-0-578-48525-6

Edited by: Katie Mac

LCG
Louisiana Cajun Girl

To my precious mom, Billie Jane Colvin Desselle, who turned out to be my biggest fan with my first book. I know she still stands by me today, coaxing me from Heaven to continue with my writing endeavor. She stood by me in good times and bad, and I know she did the best she could to raise me right. I'm everything I am today because she was there for me with love, today and every day still.

CONTENTS

CHAPTER 1

$\mathcal{I}$ walked into my apartment after another disappointing interview. As I placed my keys and purse on the side table, noise in my bedroom startled me. My mind raced as I wondered if I should call the police or find the nerves to check out the rustling.

On tiptoes, I made my way to my bedroom. Hank, my husband of four years, was rummaging through the closet.

"What are you doing here?" I said in disgust.

Several months ago, Hank had left me. Rumor was he was banging his secretary. Then a few weeks later, I was let go from an awesome job.

Hank turned to look at me. His evil sneer made my heart quiver. "This is my condo just as much as it's yours. I have every right to be here. Besides, I need casual clothes for a trip I'm taking." He pulled out several pairs of jeans and tee shirts, then eyed me up and down. "So, why are you so dressed up?"

"None of your damn business, Hank. You lost that privilege the minute you moved out," I grumbled. A sharp stab ached in my heart.

Hank walked up to me and lifted my chin, forcing me to look in his eyes. "What's wrong? Did you bomb out on another interview?"

Anger boiled over in me, and I raised my hand to slap his face. Hank grabbed my arm mid-air and gave me a crooked smirk.

"You'll never get another job. I'll be moving in here with my little angel soon. It's just a matter of time. There's one thing I have, and that's patience." Hank released my arm and stepped back. "Aw, did I hurt your little feelings?"

Blood rushed to my face as I bit my lip to hold back the tears that wanted to spill out. I wasn't about to give him the satisfaction.

"You wish, asshole," I growled.

Hank's eyebrow lifted as if he couldn't believe I'd talked back. He grabbed his clothes and pushed past me, almost knocking me down. "Move, you stupid bitch."

My emotions caused me to shake with anger as I watched him walk out the front door, cringing as it slammed shut behind him.

I slumped against the wall, falling to the ground, weak and frustrated, trying to catch my breath. My face and fingertips went numb as my chest tightened as if I was wearing a corset. The room was spinning; my hands were shaking as I tried desperately to calm my breathing. I was in a full-blown panic attack. My body slid further onto the floor until I was face down, connecting my burning skin to the cold wood floor. For what seemed like an hour, my heart struggled to return to normal.

Guilt rushed through me. How could I let that asshole control my mind and emotions to the point of losing my ability to function? The only good thing out of the day was that he was not here to witness my meltdown.

There was still time to save my life here. In a couple of days, I had two interviews back to back. Surely, one of them would hire me.

Struggling to my feet was harder than I thought. My legs were weak, and my head started to pound.

I made my way to the bed to relax only to drift off to a sound sleep.

∼

I was at the end of my wits. Hopelessness and despair were becoming a constant companion much quicker than I'd expected.

My stomach was in knots, and my hands were shaking as Mr. Simon reviewed my résumé. His expression gave nothing away, giving me no reason to expect anything other than the standard no I'd received at every other job interview the last three months.

"I'm sorry, Mrs. Hamilton, but we aren't hiring right now," he said as the paper fell to his desk, already forgotten among the clutter.

"Well, thank you for your time." Yet again, defeat washed over me as I rose from my seat. "Please keep my résumé on file for any future openings."

"Yes, I will," he said, his attention diverted to the documents on his desk.

As I walked out the door, disappointment covered me like a heavy, wet blanket. What was going on? *The Universe is squeezing the very life from me.* Squaring my shoulders, I prepared myself for one last interview before heading home. My résumé was impeccable, and I had talent beyond paper, yet no one acknowledged that.

During the drive across town, my mind spun with questions and possibilities.

My husband, Hank and I had started in advertising with the same firm, around the same time. Then several months ago, not long after he'd walked out of our marriage with the 'It's not you, it's me' speech, I lost my job. Even though I'd pulled in more revenue for the company than Hank ever did, and my education far exceeded his, he still had his job, and I didn't.

Was it because they hired me last, so I was the first to go? Was it possible someone had blackballed me? Was Hank the reason I couldn't find employment?

In a way, it made sense to my muddled mind. If I couldn't pay the rent, Hank got the condominium and everything in it. Because I believed we'd be together forever, I'd been stupid enough to let him put everything in his name while I made payments.

Hank would benefit immensely if I lost everything.

Would he stoop so low as to make sure I wasn't hired anywhere? Did he have enough pull to keep me from getting a new job?

As I walked into the twenty-story building, my confidence grew. My application and résumé spoke for itself, and I would get this job.

I had to.

"My name is Sarah Hamilton, and I have an appointment at two with Mr. Nelson," I said to the receptionist with a smile as I signed in.

"Oh, Mrs. Hamilton, I've been trying to call you all morning to save you a trip. The company has hired internally, so we have no openings at this time."

My face fell, my confidence draining. Again.

"Please keep my résumé on file for future openings," I said in the mechanical voice I used at each failed interview.

"Sure will, Mrs. Hamilton. Have a nice day."

Have a nice day! Was she kidding me?

My life had suddenly taken a nosedive. In such a short time, I'd lost my husband and the best paying job I'd ever had. I had been happy living life to the fullest in an expensive condominium located in the best part of town.

What the hell had happened?

Deep in thought, I entered my tenth story condominium. Standing at the door of the entryway, I gazed at the floor-to-ceiling windows that stretched across two walls of the living room, giving me the perfect view of the city, New York City. They made the room look bright and spacious. The other walls were a pale gray that accented the ceiling light. The furniture was modern cream tones with coffee-colored throw pillows. The long wooden table with dark gray, high-back chairs fit perfectly against the far wall between the windows and kitchen.

Hank and I had each kept one piece of furniture from our younger days to remind us how far we had come. His was an antique, dark mahogany table he said his great-grandfather had made. I threw my keys on it along with my purse. My piece of furniture was Old Blue, a recliner from my college days. I kicked off my heels in the corner by the door, walked over, and flopped down on it, broken-hearted by another rejection.

Total, utter exhaustion and loss shrouded me to the point of overload. Tears ran down my face, streaking my make-up and plugging my nose.

Time was running out. There were only a couple of weeks left to get my life in order. The eviction notice was expected any day since I was several months late on rent, and those interviews were the last leads I had on a job. What would I do, and where would I go?

Please, God, help me.

For a fleeting moment, I wondered if life was worth all the heartache and struggle. Maybe I would be better off if I ended it all.

It's not like I could run home to Mom and Dad. Those days were over, really over. It had been five years since they'd passed on to the great unknown, leaving me alone, with no siblings.

I sobbed into the cushion until a light knock at the door caught my attention.

"Great! I can't even cry in peace." Sniffing, I grabbed a tissue and blew my nose as I dragged myself to the door.

A glance through the peephole revealed the mail carrier. What did he want? Couldn't he just leave me alone so I could finish my pity party?

Though I didn't want to, I cracked open the door. "Can I-- I h-help you?" I stammered, my breath catching in my throat. In my mind, I was screaming profanity from the pits of hell for the interruption.

"Need you to sign for this," he said in a gentle voice of concern as he searched my face.

Sticking the letter under my arm, I signed the green card, shoved it through the crack, and closed the door.

"Must be mail-ordered, divorce papers," I grumbled under my breath, too depressed to care.

No way was I letting a certified letter distract me from my self-absorbed party of one. That's when I noticed my red swollen eyes. No wonder the mail carrier was looking at me so intently. I threw the letter on the side table next to the keys to the new black, shiny BMW I was about to lose, too. That thought made me wail even more. Everything I'd worked for would soon be gone.

"My credit score'll plummet to the center of the

Earth and be burned to smithereens in the lava." My frustration released in a loud yell.

My stuck-up friends with their nose in the air, those I thought would stand by me, had given me the cold shoulder since I'd lost my high-paying job. Even my prayer partners at the huge church, where everyone who was anyone went—only the elite, crème de la crème type people—were nice to my face. But out of the corner of my eye, I caught their smug looks, as if I was in the wrong place. Maybe I wasn't good enough or rich enough anymore to set foot in their precious church.

"Who needs them?" Anger welled up inside me.

My time was up. So, what do I do? Give up and throw in the towel? Do I settle for a piece of shit job and move into low-income housing?

I screamed at the top of my lungs, so loud the neighbors probably heard.

"But no, they're not home. They have jobs."

Looking around the room, I realized nothing except the recliner was mine. Everything else was new, rented, or belonged to that piece of shit husband who was waiting for me to fall flat on my face and lose it all so he could move in with his mistress.

My mouth felt like sandpaper, so I went to get a bottled water from the state-of-the-art, stainless steel refrigerator. Standing there with the French-doors wide open, I realized the shelves were bare, except for two sweet baby Gherkins floating in a jar and a slice of cheese. Shocked, I hurried to the butler's pantry and found two pouches of tuna and a can of spinach.

"Where's all the food? Have I been so self-absorbed that I forgot to buy groceries? Well, at least I don't have much of an appetite, thanks to all the worry and stress." Reluctantly, I grabbed a glass from the drainboard and filled it. "I'm reduced to drinking tap water. Oh my god, what did I do to deserve this?"

The window overlooking the city I loved drew me to it. Lights were turning on one by one, making everything look like a carpet of stars. Never had I felt so happy, living in the wealthiest part of town. Eating at the best restaurants and shopping in the high-end areas was the life I had always wanted.

There had to be an answer so I could stay. My heart was breaking at the thought of leaving it all behind.

With my shoulders slumped in defeat, I crept back to my recliner, tears streaming down my face, curled up, folding my hands over my heart, and whispered a prayer.

"What do I do now, Lord?"

Dark shadows appeared on the wall and ceiling. Blotting the tissue at my eyes, I leaned back further. My heart rate slowed, and I tried to clear my mind, concentrating on the dark silhouettes stretched across the room. The shadows took on the shape of an angel, pointing towards the front door. *How strange.*

"If only there were real angels who could help me out of this mess. Wouldn't that be nice?" My eyes squinted at the shape. "Yep, the angel's still there." My voice faded to a whisper.

Closing my eyes for the last time, I drifted off to where life always seemed easier.

~

*W*hen I woke, the first thing I did was check the voice mail, hoping someone had called me back about a job. There was nothing, no blinking light, no chance in hell I would be able to pay for all the stuff. With sadness in my heart, I picked up the receiver to make sure the phone was still working and found the usual buzzing noise.

"Well, at least they haven't turned off the phone, yet."

Disappointment invaded my mind and heart again, leaving me paralyzed with fear. My body shook, and I wondered if soaking in a long, hot bath and changing my clothes would put me in a better frame of mind and give me a better outlook on the day.

As I listened to the water filling the tub, I examined my puffy eyes and streaked make-up. While trying to detangle my hair with my fingers, the mirror fogged. I walked across the bathroom into a wall of mist.

I eased into the hot water and relaxed against the back of the tub, trying to let go of my doubts and fears of the future. The steam thickened like pea soup. Leaning forward to turn off the water, I noticed an outline in the floor-length mirror attached to the bathroom door. Wiping my eyes, I searched the bathroom.

"Who's there?" I asked my heart racing.

The room took on an unusual glow. I gripped the

edge of the Jacuzzi tub, my breath catching in my throat, trying to focus on the figure. My mouth gaped as I gazed at the beauty before me. My fingers released the rim as peace fell on me like rain in the garden.

"This can't be," I whispered.

The figure appeared to be a female with long, blonde hair cascading to her waist. She wore a luminous gown of glowing white light, which reflected off the mirrors and mist like a sea of tiny diamonds.

"Why are you here?" I managed to ask.

Her reply was to smile with such love that all I could do was smile back. Every negative thought disappeared from my head.

As I looked upon her beauty, she slowly faded away, taking the light with her, and leaving the dullness of this world behind. Though she was gone, the peace remained. Her appearance took away every ounce of fear, making me feel that somehow everything would be okay.

Sure, I went to church, but there was never a bond or closeness with God. It was more like show-and-tell on Sunday. Who had the most money, gave the most, and came to church with the fanciest car and clothes? I wondered if maybe I was missing something in my life, something of the spiritual nature.

Then it hit me. The vision I saw last night. Didn't I see the silhouette of an angel?

"She pointed to the front door." Curious and excited, I jumped from the tub and grabbed a towel, wrapping it around me as I exited the bathroom. Slipping across the hardwood floors, skidding into the opposite wall, I then slid down the hall, leaving a soapy trail to the front door. Looking around, I saw nothing.

Out of breath, I tried to recall exactly what had happened. Okay, I was sitting in my recliner. No, I was resting in my recliner, when she appeared.

"What did she want me to see?"

Maybe it was a shadow of something in the room. I went from one side to the other but found nothing.

"With all the stress lately, I'm losing my mind on top of everything else. I can just add it to the list of other things I've lost." Gritting my teeth in frustration, I figured I shouldn't have drunk that tap water the day before.

Analyzing the situation, I was certain it was an angelic being of some kind. It was a dark silhouette pointing towards the front door. Clutching the towel, I walked closer to the spot, picked up the keys and my purse, and moved an ornamental vase.

Wait! The letter! I walked to my recliner, sat down, and opened the envelope.

When I finished reading it, my mouth dropped open in shock. The paper slipped from my shaky fingers to the floor.

"It can't be. No way, no way!"

After a second or two, I picked it up to examine it closer. The letterhead from the Office of Brian Thibodeaux, Attorney at Law, looked authentic. I reread it a couple of times. After a minute or two, the truth broke through the shock.

How was I lucky enough to have inherited a house from a relative I didn't even know I had?

"Well, angels, guess you were telling me my next move."

I can do this, right? I'll pack some of my clothes, and just go, right? Start over in . . . I re-read the heading. *Marksville, Louisiana?*

Where in the world was Marksville, Louisiana?

Could it be some kind of scam, fraud, or swindle? There was only one way to find out. I jumped from my chair, grabbed my phone, and with a slight clearing of my throat, made the call.

"Yes, hello, this is Sarah Hamilton. I'm calling about the letter I received in the mail." I held my breath as the receptionist talked, wondering if she was going to tell me I'd inherited a house at the low cost of a million dollars. But no, I wasn't even close. "Yes, ma'am. Yes, I can be there middle of next week. Ok, sure, two o'clock, Wednesday."

She disconnected the call, and I stared at my phone, dumbfounded.

It looked like I was going to Louisiana.

∼

*O*ver the next several days, I sold my BMW to a rich neighbor who wanted to surprise his wife. He had admired my car from the day I'd pulled into the garage. I didn't get much money for it since I owed a lifetime on it, but several thousand dollars bought me another one. It wasn't as nice, but at least it would get me where I wanted to go.

Since the used car only had room for three or four suitcases, I was forced to part with most of my designer clothing. Every time I sold something, it was like a stab in my heart, but there was also a sense of relief and lightness. Of course, I wasn't stupid enough to get rid of everything. I kept a couple of suits for work, a fancy dinner dress, and enough high-priced clothes to maintain my dignity.

The stainless steel appliances were new enough to return with my excuse, that they didn't go with my décor. As I went through the condo, everything that had a receipt, I exchanged for cash. Since Hank left me holding the bag, I was going to render his plans null and void in any way I could.

By the end of the fourth day, everything was taken care of. I realized luck was definitely with me. On the other hand, was it divine intervention?

There was only one tiny issue to handle before I left.

The hardest and scariest thing I'd ever have to do.

I needed to confront Hank and give in. He won. He got the condo and everything in it.

Well, at least what was left.

How I wished I could see his face when he walked in there and saw it almost bare. Yep, all his precious, had-to-have items were gone.

I couldn't help but smile as I realized I got the last laugh after all.

I tried all morning to get an appointment with my

husband, but his stubborn, self-centered girlfriend gave me one excuse after another.

Therefore, I dressed in my finest outfit and drove over to confront Hank.

With my head high, I walked in and approached his secretary. I didn't remember her being so beautiful. She had straight, long, blonde hair, sky-blue eyes, and a creamy, unblemished complexion.

Swallowing hard, I tried to speak.

No wonder he left me. She looks like she belongs on the cover of a magazine.

"Can I help you?" she said as she turned around from a phone call. Her smile faded as she recognized me and gave me a disgusted look from head to toe.

"I'm here to see my husband," I said with authority.

She stood, and I felt small next to her tall, slender figure. My five-foot-four was nothing compared to her stature.

"As I said on the phone, he's not available," she said in a condescending tone.

I shook with anger. If she thought she would turn me away, I'd jump over the desk and pull her hair out.

"Well, not available won't do," I said as I walked past her desk into Hank's office and found it empty.

"As I said, he's not available," she repeated.

"Listen here, you bleached, blonde bimbo." I put my face inches from hers. "Not available and out of the office are two different things. Do you hear me? Where is he?"

"He's, he's out of town at a conference," she stuttered.

Out of town, my ass.

"You could have saved us both a lot of time and effort if you had said that on the phone."

I stormed out the office, wondering how this dumb blonde got a job there in the first place. After the run-in with Hank's girlfriend, the more I liked the idea of leaving the condominium with the late charges and empty of most of Hank's precious furniture.

To make things more difficult for him, I ordered the locks changed, too. It was my nature not to give in to a fight, especially one I didn't start.

So, come morning, I would pack my things in my second-hand car, plug in my GPS, and head to the land of the unknown.

I bit my nail as the dreaded fear gripped me again. What if I got lost, broke down, or heaven help me, was hijacked by a junky wanting sexual favors? I giggled. Stress was making me giddy.

Then I remembered the angelic vision and the inheritance.

Calm down, Sarah. Everything will be okay. Remember, you have angelic help.

At that thought, I knew there was something higher working in my life that wouldn't possibly steer me wrong.

It was hard sleeping on folded blankets on the floor, tossing and turning, but as much as I loved that bed, the money I received from its sale made it worthwhile.

Early the next morning, I loaded my car with boxes, suitcases, and my recliner, then made my way upstairs for one last look. As I gazed from wall to wall, I realized I really had no right to anything else. I stopped for one last look at what I had had. With tears in my eyes and an ache in my heart, I closed the door one final time on the most wonderful place in the world.

I couldn't believe I was walking away from the life I'd worked so hard for. By the time Hank realized I'd left, and all his prized possessions were gone, it would piss him off immensely. My tears were replaced with giggles as I walked to my car.

With my destination loaded in the GPS, and maps by my side for backup, I headed out of the garage and said goodbye to New York. I used my rearview mirror for one final glance at the city I loved. How I would miss it all.

Well, all but Hank.

CHAPTER 2

Time dragged on like a bad movie as I passed through one city after another. How many days would it take to get to the sweat-lands of Louisiana? I was dreading the swamps but felt there was a purpose behind the move. As I drove and drove, the cities got smaller, and the buildings got shorter.

Eventually, the cities were replaced by pastures, farmland, and an endless spread of trees. Everywhere I went, there was a continuous line of nothingness. Boring, boring, boring. How could people live like this? What did these people do for fun?

Why was I traveling across the country to a state that rates one of the lowest in education and jobs, and high in cancer and obesity? What was wrong with me?

After several wrong turns to places I couldn't find on the map, living out my car, and eating Happy Meals with gallons of coffee, I arrived late in Marksville, a place I would rather have passed through.

I couldn't believe my eyes. The small town, population five thousand, seven hundred, and two people wasn't a city compared to New York's population of over eight million. It was barely a period on a piece of paper.

Too exhausted to think anymore, I found a room at the casino right off Highway One. They happened to be running a special for out-of-towners. I was sure out-of-town and probably out of my mind. Giggling, I wondered if I could get a discount for that, too.

After check-in, I dropped my suitcases inside the doorway. After spending so much time trying to sleep in that old car, I didn't care where I was or what the room looked like. I had tunnel vision, and all I saw was a bed.

~

J woke feeling like a dazed zombie.

After a minute or two sitting there confused, it came back to me.

"Oh yeah, I'm in Lousy-Ana." I moaned in disgust.

Rubbing my eyes, I dragged my tired body to the curtains. At the sight before me, I felt like someone had slapped me. My room faced the woods.

"Oh my God, more trees," I said, gritting my teeth.

I looked at my watch; it was ten after ten. Wow, I had slept over sixteen hours. I had plenty of time for a quick shower and breakfast before I needed to be at the lawyers.

Turned out, the breakfast cost more than I wanted to

spend, so I settled for the complimentary coffee. There was no telling how many days the process of inheriting a house would take. My biggest concern was it might not be worth my trouble, and I'd need money to get back to New York.

"New York? I have nothing left in New York." Loss filled my heart as I ached for the only life I'd ever known.

To clear my mind, I went for a walk. One last look at my reflection in the souvenir shop's glass had me smiling. My long brown wavy hair, green eyes, and creamy complexion looked awesome after a good night's sleep. The trails behind the casino produced a wooden bridge over a stream. I was so thankful I didn't have to touch anything. Nestled among the trees was a variety of birds I'd never seen before. Then again, the only birds I saw in the city were pigeons.

When the time came to leave for the meeting, I was more than a little relieved to leave nature behind. Following the GPS directions, I found the office. Adjusting my jacket and top, I flipped my hair off my shoulder and entered the building, thankful to be getting out of the heat and humidity.

I signed in at the empty front desk, had a seat, and waited to be called. A quick glance around led me to question if this was a lawyer's office. The furniture was worn but usable, mismatched, and resembled something found on a curbside in New York. *Well, we're not in New York anymore, Toto.* Funny, I didn't think over the rainbow would be in such a poor location.

"Miss Hamilton, please follow me." A young girl of about twenty brought me back to reality. She escorted me into an office that looked like the rest of the place, dull and secondhand.

A middle-aged man with thick, dark rimmed-glasses and dark eyes stood from behind the desk and extended his hand to greet me. He was tall and slim, and I couldn't stop noticing how the oily bald spot shone beneath the long, thin strands of his dark hair. His scent was almost overpowering as though he'd added cologne before I'd walked in his office. He was wearing a freshly pressed jacket and matching pants, a starched high-neck collared shirt, and coordinating tie. I got the impression he was trying a little too hard to impress me.

"Miss Hamilton, it's great to meet you. I'm Brian Thibodeaux," he said, his accent thick as honey.

"Yes, nice to meet you." My voice came out curt and short, evidence of my nerves. My hands were sweating, and I was hoping the long trip wasn't for nothing.

"Please, have a seat." He pointed to two chairs in front of his desk.

Finding a comfortable spot on the lumpy cushion took a few seconds. While Mr. Thibodeaux searched through the papers and folders on his desk, I used the time to inspect his office. The wall behind him was full of thick leather-bound books and a framed law degree certificate.

Hmm, guess he was the real deal unless the paper was a fake. With the mismatched secondhand furniture and a layer of dust on his desk, I couldn't help but wonder if the lack I saw around me had anything to do with his ability to work on my inheritance case.

"May I see two forms of identification?" he asked, clearing his throat.

Thankful I remembered to keep my important papers with me, I dug in my purse for my birth certificate and driver's license.

Mr. Thibodeaux had his face down, reading something in a folder. I cleared my throat to get his attention so I could hand him my ID.

He lifted his hand without raising his head. What was wrong with him? I slapped the papers in his hand to get his attention with no response.

With the thickness of his glasses and his closeness to the pages, I concluded he had bad eyes and probably needed to examine the papers closely.

He studied my documents. "Okay, it looks like you're definitely the heir of this estate." He finally raised his head and asked, "Did you know Pauline Bordelon, your mom's half-sister?"

"Honestly, I didn't know my mom had any siblings. This has all been a shock to me."

"Well, it seems your grandfather was stationed here at Fort Polk, where he met a young Cajun girl before your grandmother. Need I say more?" Mr. Thibodeaux said as he walked around the desk to sit beside me.

"No, I get the gist." The news shocked me, compounding the uncomfortable feeling of being so close to this man.

"Well, Miss Hamilton—" he leaned closer, putting his

hand on the arm of the chair, but I jerked from his attempted touch "—I'm not sure how Pauline knew about your mom, or how much she knew about you, but if you're agreeable, I can research it more."

"No, no, don't bother. It doesn't matter now, anyway, does it?" His forward action made my skin crawl. After such a long trip and everything that had happened in the last several weeks, my mind was stuck on pause, and I found it hard to respond with any kind of appropriate action like remorse. "When did you say she died?"

"Well, actually, she was declared dead several weeks ago, about the time we sent you your first letter."

"Excuse me? Did I hear you right? Where's she buried?"

"There's a grave marker behind the house."

My heart skipped a beat in shock. Who in their right mind put a headstone in their backyard?

"Brian, where's the body? There *is* a body, right?"

"Well, no. Actually, she was reported missing a long time ago. Neighbors witnessed her taking her boat out in Spring Bayou, and she never came back. After weeks of searching, the police found her half-sunken boat, so they called off the search party, declaring she was dead, maybe eaten by an alligator, or something." Brian walked to his chair, leaning back and sighing. "After an extensive search of the house, we located her will and found that you are the only living relative to Ms. Pauline. Your location was on some papers we found."

All the information Brian was telling me left me

dazed, almost dizzy. It seemed so strange, the coincidence of it landing in my lap when I needed it most.

"So, here's a check for two thousand dollars and the keys to your new place."

"Money!" I said shocked with my eyes bugged out.

"Yes, you have an allowance of two thousand a month for the rest of your life."

My purse fell to the floor as I reached for the check. "I, uh, I didn't realize . . . there was money too."

"In these parts, we'd consider your aunt wealthy." Brian cleared his throat to cover a laugh. "She was a bit eccentric and very tight with her money, as you'll soon see. Well, okay, just sign these papers, and I'll drive you out since you're not familiar with the area."

"Thank you, I'd appreciate that," was out of my mouth before I realized what I said. My heart was happy someone could show me around, but why did it have to be him?

CHAPTER 3

We left my car in the parking lot. Brian said it was not far, and we could pick it up later. As we drove to the residence, I decided it was too quiet and started a conversation to pass the time.

"I'm not really a nature person, so it's going to take me a little while to get used to all these trees and streams."

Brian gave me a strange look. "Did you say you're not a nature girl?"

"Well, no, I was brought up in New York City. The closest I've come to trees and nature is the park I went to as a child."

Brian laughed and said under his breath, "This is going to be good."

"Excuse me?" I asked, annoyed at his comment. My eyes widened. Was he making fun of me?

"I don't know how to tell you this, but first, we don't have streams here. We have bayous. Second, your new house isn't exactly in the center of town. In fact, it has nature all around it. There's a small bayou on one side, and your backyard is called Spring Bayou. Spring Bayou is well known for its beauty and great fishing. If you're not a nature girl, then you better get some rubber boots, because you're about to get a firsthand lesson in nature."

My mouth fell open. *Oh no, what have I gotten myself into? How will I survive when I don't like touching greenery, much less living in it?*

My mind went to my childhood where my mother had always said nature was to look at, not to touch. Mom had always kept an impeccable house, and everything had to be clean and orderly. Nature stayed outside, not on her floors.

"I'm sure it'll be ok." I lied, trying to be optimistic, considering I had nowhere else to go.

The road started out, lined with houses, but further along, it was wall-to-wall trees. I really got worried when the asphalt turned to gravel. Oh my, it was worse than I'd thought.

He wasn't lying when he said it was in nature. Fear crept into my heart and mind. My hands shook, and my throat started to close. If I didn't get a hold on my emotions, panic would take over. I took a deep breath.

"Are-Are you sure you took the right road?" I asked, hoping not.

Brian's eyebrow lifted as his lips parted, showing his crooked yellow teeth.

He slowed the car to a crawl as we drove over a cattle

guard. My hands gripped my purse in anticipation of what I would find.

Once we cleared the thick, unkempt fence line, my mouth fell open. Someone had cleared the land and mowed the grass. Along, the left side of the dirt road was a line of huge beautiful trees lining the driveway like the ones at my childhood park. For a second, the scenery reminded me of a movie. I couldn't remember what movie, but the beauty awed me.

As we drove closer to the house, the beautiful trees were replaced by scary-looking ones, lining a body of water. An abundant amount of moss, hung loosely from the limbs, giving an eerie look about the place.

I guessed this was the Spring Bayou Brian was talking about.

"Well, this is it," Brian announced as we stopped in front of a large two-story house.

Steps led to a porch the length of the front. While it desperately needed repair and paint, it looked livable.

Cascading across the front railing were overgrown bushes with beautiful light blues and purplish flowers, intermingled with weeds and dead stalks. The landscape was in desperate need of maintenance. The porch held three rocking chairs on the left. A large planter lay on its side by the front door, spilling dirt and the dead, dried stems of what I imagined was once a beautiful flowering plant.

"You'll need a good carpenter. With some paint and repairs, this place would really look nice, especially with the swamp behind the house making an excellent backdrop of naaaturrre." Brian drew out the word nature with a smile that looked somewhat evil.

I didn't like this man and his attitude. It was as if he wanted to scare me off, or have me give up, go home, and just leave my inheritance. A shiver ran up my spine.

"You're not cold, are you? It's ninety-five degrees today, with a humidity of eighty-five percent."

"No, it's like someone walked over my grave."

"I haven't heard that expression in a long time." Brian smiled. "Ready to see the inside?"

When I nodded, Brian got out, walked around the car, and opened the door for me. As I exited, Brian took the keys from my clutched hand, and I followed him. My mind released the fear and replaced it with the disappointment of the sight before me.

"It's Victorian style, popular for the south," Brian said as he led me up the steps.

Houses like this didn't exist in the New York I knew, and it didn't fit the plantation type I'd seen in books and movies. My eyes went from the porch to the three sets of windows on the second floor. Faded grayish shutters framed them, some hanging lopsided by a single screw. Through the dirty glass were torn, faded drapes. The white paint was peeling, and the siding boards were loose in several places.

The place might be something special for this part of the country, but it looked like a dump to me.

Brian cleared his throat, and I realized I was gawking with my mouth opened, while he waited by the front door. Coming back to the present, I rushed up the stairs.

As he turned the handle and opened the door, it squealed, in desperate need of oil.

We entered the residence, and my mouth fell. There were thick spider webs hanging from the ceiling and corners and leaves on the floor near a broken window. It was old and musty with a thick layer of dust on a bunch of old antiques. It was as if Aunt Pauline had moved into a furnished house from the eighteen-hundreds and bought nothing new for the rest of her life. From the light fixtures to the paintings on the wall, everything was outdated.

I was appalled at all the dirt and grime, but eager to find some rubber gloves and get everything clean and in order. As we walked through the house, I took a mental note of the supplies I would need before I moved my things. I grabbed a tissue from my purse to cover my hand so I wouldn't have to touch anything. The hallway door, which I thought led to the cellar, was actually a closet.

"Wow, that's unusual."

"What's that?" Brian asked.

"This house doesn't have a basement."

"Most houses in Louisiana, at least the southern part, rarely have basements. It's too damp. That's also why most people here are buried above ground. Just depends on the area. New Orleans is below sea level, and they have to bury above ground. This house is so close to the swamps, there'd be several feet of water in your cellar if you dug one." Brian peeked out one of the curtains. "If you'd like, Miss Sarah, when we finish up here, we can set up an account at the bank in town, go to the post office, and make phone calls to get your utilities turned on."

"Thanks. That would be great." I was very surprised he would go out of his way. He was a lawyer. Didn't he have work to do? As much as I appreciated his help, I couldn't help but feel he was a busybody and wanted to nose around in my business. I was very suspicious of Brian's motive for helping me. "By the way, I'm Mrs., not Miss."

"Excuse me," Brian said somewhat sarcastically.

"You and your receptionist called me Miss Sarah. I'm Mrs."

Brian looked at me strangely. I wasn't sure if I offended him because I corrected him, or if he knew I was a Mrs. and calling everyone Miss is just a way of the south.

"Oh. Will your husband be joining you soon?"

"We're separated, at present, so no." Not sure why, but I felt embarrassed to admit I didn't have a husband coming, or why I felt the need to tell him I was separated.

"I don't mean to add to your worries, but this state is a community property state, so now you may be looking at sharing this with your husband if you ever get divorced."

Oh my, that's all I needed. It didn't even cross my mind I might have to share my inheritance with Hank. My house, my money, and the condo?

I peered out a back window and noticed the grave

marker. "Brian, may I ask why Pauline's grave marker is in the backyard and not in a cemetery?"

"Well, she wasn't a member of any Church in the area, and well, she was kind of touched."

"Touched?" I asked, dumbfounded.

"What I mean is her butter slid off the toast."

I glared at him as if he had two heads.

"You know, a brick short of a load, not the brightest crayon in the box, her elevator—"

"Okay, okay, I get it." I had to turn, so he didn't see my grin. He was a lawyer, for goodness' sake, yet he was talking like an uneducated idiot. I shook my head; certain he wouldn't last two seconds in New York.

The rest of the day went well. With Brian's help, I got my banking done and my mailing address updated. Because of the time, the utilities wouldn't be turned on until the next day. It didn't matter. I was moving in, with or without electricity.

Brian suggested I stay another night at the casino. He knew a man who knew another man who worked at the casino and pulled a few strings to get me a night free due to my hardship. Who could pass up a free night at the casino? Compared to staying at an old house in the swamps, I felt lucky. The casino was great. It had everything you could imagine in there. It reminded me of a cruise ship where you could eat, sleep, shop, swim, and be entertained by a movie or live bands, all in one place.

The hospitality was awesome. The young man who'd checked me in the first night, Ronald, was so genuine and down to earth that I felt happy to have met him.

I had to admit the people in Lousy-Ana were a lot nicer than I'd thought. Maybe it wasn't so lousy after all.

Besides nature, swamps, and heat, I decided that the new chapter in my life would probably be good. With my finger's crossed, I kissed them and thanked God for this new start.

CHAPTER 4

*N*ext morning, I was bright-eyed and bushy-tailed and excited to be leaving the casino. Ronald's smiling face as he told me goodbye was like seeing an old friend.

As I checked out for the last time, hope for a wonderful, new beginning blossomed inside me. With anticipation in one pocket and fear in the other, I left the comfort of the casino.

The sun's rays hit me like a ton of bricks, and there wasn't a cloud in the sky to help shade the blinding light. My God, it was hot. It wasn't like a regular heat. The air was so thick; I felt like I had to push my way through it. The worst thing, it was only nine AM. What in the world would it be like by the afternoon?

Despite the heat, I was excited about being settled into my new old house.

My optimism came from me preaching to myself continually that *I can do this, it's not out of my comfort zone,* and *everything will work out.* Those sayings went around and around in my head like a merry-go-round.

Walking up the steps of my newly gained house gave me chills up and down my spine as it had done the previous day. I wondered if it would be an everyday feeling, or if it was because I dreaded walking into all the filth and grime. Being surrounded by awful nature with the thought of the crud touching me didn't help matters.

That sensation of someone walking over my grave gave me a feeling of dread. What if it was a warning of impending doom? I laughed at myself for being so scared of being out of my comfort zone.

"I'll just say my mantra again and everything will be all right," I said, crossing my fingers behind my back.

Standing in the open doorway, I looked at the cleaning job and said a quick prayer.

"Lord, you know I don't like dirt. Please, protect me." I snickered. Taking two steps in, I looked to my left and flipped the light switch. "Just great, just freaking great, the electricity isn't on. They better get those lights turned on soon," I mumbled under my breath. I placed my bags on the bottom step of the staircase and walked to the kitchen to see if the water was on. "Well, thank you, God, for water."

Okay, first thing on my list from the store was bottled water. I never wanted to drink regular tap again. I was happy with myself for thinking ahead and hiding several bottles from the casino in my suitcase.

I sighed. At least I had water to clean the filthy

house. It felt overwhelming. It wasn't a two-bedroom condo. No, it was a four-bedroom house, with a living room, dining room, a large kitchen, and a bathroom.

The walls were skinny strips of painted wood, not like the drywall I was accustomed to. The only difference from room to room was the paint color. The lofty ceilings were a lighter white and framed with large crown molding.

I claimed the downstairs bedroom as mine and hoped cleaning only the first floor would leave me time to explore the town and buy food.

The stifling heat got the best of me, so I opened as many windows as I could, propping each one up with a stick.

In the kitchen, an overwhelming, disgusting smell made me want to gag and run for the door. It had to be coming from the refrigerator. Standing back, I eased it open and heaved, closing it immediately. After a few minutes arguing with myself, I decided it had to be dealt with, no matter how much it grossed me out.

Under the kitchen sink was an unopened box of rubber gloves and cleaning supplies, just what I needed to tackle the dreadful mess.

I twisted my hair up, pinned it with a barrette, and went to work, pushing and pulling the small refrigerator out the back door. The black, moldy food was unrecognizable. With a large garbage can close to the edge of the porch, I found a small shovel to scrape the putrid mess into. I then hooked up the hose by the back steps and washed it down. Using a spray bottle of cleaning solution, I saturated the refrigerator inside and out, leaving the door open for airing out when I finished.

My next challenge was the pantry. Aunt Pauline seemed to have just about everything I needed in the kitchen except the perishable food like coffee, bread, crackers, and frozen stuff.

As long as I concentrated on the task at hand, I managed to forget all the dirt. Before long, the whole kitchen was clean and organized as an accountant's ledger.

When I went into the bathroom, I froze in shock. Against the far wall, under the window, was an awesome clawfoot tub that astounded me. In New York, an original antique clawfoot tub would go for thousands of dollars, and I had one of my own. How jealous the office girls would be if they saw it. I couldn't wait to get my first bath.

To the right, a pipe went up the wall to an old shower head protruding above a small round rod with a molded shower curtain hanging from it. Close to the tub was a round, white, antique sink with a small square mirror above it. Behind the bathroom door were cabinets that held towels, toilet paper, and other bathroom products. I pulled up my sleeves and went to work.

The final touch was my old blue recliner. In two trips, I carried my one precious piece of furniture in and assembled it in the living room. I looked around, realizing I actually had a house full of furniture that was mine.

"I own a house; I own furniture."

Being busy, time passed faster than I'd expected. With everything done, I cleaned up, changed my clothes, and headed for the store before it got too late.

Brian was right. The house could and would really look nice once I fixed it up.

In my mind, I was picturing it gracing the cover of Home and Garden, when footsteps on the back porch and a light knock interrupted my fantasy.

Who in the world would come to the back door? That wasn't proper at all.

Part of me hesitated, but I was in the country, not the city. It was probably nothing to be afraid of.

I reached the back door and opened it. Hmm.

"Hello, anyone there?"

Nothing but the leaves moving on the trees. Well, maybe they walked to the front door like they're supposed to. When I got around the house, though, there was no car or anything moving. Feeling somewhat strange, I walked back to the backyard and towards the...

"What did Brian call this water? Oh, yeah, by-you. Bayou? What an odd name."

The sun streaked through the leaves like a light show. It was quiet and peaceful, but a little eerie with the moss hanging thick in most of the trees.

"Oh wow, there's a dock. How cool is that?" I said with sarcasm and rolling my eyes.

The dock was in desperate need of repair like everything else. With a couple of new boards and maybe, some paint, it could be useable for someone, not me mind you.

I thought it strange that a boat was tied to the dock. I thought no one was there. Oh, maybe it was Aunt Pauline's boat. No, didn't Brian tell me her boat sank? I retreated. Someone must be here. Turning to run back to the house, I crashed into a tree, knocking me backward.

"Oh my God, where did that come from?" With total embarrassment, like an idiot, I looked to see if anyone saw me, then ran back to the house. I slammed the door and locked it, then laid my head against it and smiled. Who would see me out there in the jungles of Louisiana, anyway?

I'm sure that boat was there all along, and I'm just losing it, and the knock was probably a limb hitting the house or an acorn falling on the tin roof.

Somewhat spooked, I grabbed my keys and purse and rushed out the front door. Did I want to spend the night there, alone? Was I in over my head, camping-out in the boonies? What I wanted more than anything was to forget the grocery store and drive back to New York to my elegant condo.

Sadness filled my heart. I could never go back to my wonderful condo. It was lost forever, and I was stuck in a little town with no friends or family. Loneliness fell on me like darkness. I'd never felt lonely in New York. Thousands of people were there. How could anyone be alone when several feet from in any direction was always someone to be found? Marksville, Louisiana was different. I was at the end of a dead-end street with not a human in sight.

After what seemed like forever, I reached the main highway and looked around with disgust.

The town wasn't much, and definitely didn't fit my upper-class way of doing things. Oh, great lucky me. There was a Walmart to buy groceries, not like my kind of store. I would never set foot in one in New York, but you did what you had to do under horrendous conditions.

Just go in, get what I have to, and get out.

It was actually somewhat convenient to shop so close to Aunt Pauline's house and not have to fight traffic and loads of people.

Everyone had an accent like Brian. An old couple was speaking a form of French, what I assumed was the basic Cajun language. Who knew? Guess I needed to brush up on my history.

The people dressed differently. Women wore old jeans or stretch pants and tee shirts with tennis shoes. In a public store, no less. The casual work-in-the-yard type of clothes was totally out of fashion, and not one woman had on heels.

The men were the worst. Some were dirty and unkempt and looked like they hadn't shaved in months. Some had puffy lips or a growth in their cheeks. One man, in particular, had the nerve to spit the most disgusting brown slime into an empty Coke bottle. I couldn't help but gag.

A couple of men were clean-shaven and dressed

plainly in tee shirts and blue jeans, but the guy in camouflage pants, a torn green shirt, and some kind of muddy work boots must have just come in from hunting.

I couldn't believe no one wore dress pants or designer shirts.

Since I didn't want to stay any longer than necessary, I finished shopping in record time. When I got back to the house and carried in my groceries, I found I'd left in such a hurry, I'd forgotten to lock the front door.

Oh my God, if I had done that in New York, I wouldn't have anything left in my condo. I hadn't been there one day, and I was acting irresponsibly.

After eating, I was in the living room, and once more, I heard footsteps on the back porch, followed by a small knock.

I jumped up and ran to check. Again, no one was there. It was pitch black and spooky outside. I closed the door, confused and shaken by the weird noises.

Since the sun was gone, and I felt paranoid in a strange house, I ran around making sure every window and door was closed and locked.

I tried the light switch, hoping something had changed but wasn't surprised when nothing happened.

"Well, I guess roughing it for one night won't kill me."

I found some candles and an old lamp with a clear liquid in it. Before long, I had the whole downstairs full of light.

Since there was no electricity to wash sheets, I made

do and grabbed some from the bedroom closet. I knew they had to be dusty but at least they didn't have human body cells on it, even if Pauline and I were related.

The air was stagnating and humid. All the Clorox in Walmart would never get the musty, mildewed smell out this old house.

CHAPTER 5

*O*utside was pitch black. No street lights, no moon, no animal or insect sounds. Nothing but darkness thick enough to cut with a knife.

As I prepared for bed, I reluctantly half-opened the nearest window to get some air. Maybe I should have stayed at the casino one more night.

To me, there was nothing worse than a strange bed, in a strange house, in the middle of swamp country. Perspiration dripped down my face and neck and pooled under my breasts. Tossing and turning drove home how desperately I wanted to be back in my cool, clean condo. Right around that time of night, I would be looking out over the city while sipping a glass of wine, admiring the flickering lights, and knowing the city was alive with energy.

In the middle of the bayou, it was dead and immensely dark. The dead wasn't because of the humid weather or lack of breeze or light. Instead, it was an overwhelming dead, dark, thick void. In fact, it was somewhat depressing. I felt a need to cry but was just too exhausted after such a long day.

Around one AM, the temperature dropped enough for me to drift off to sleep until a noise shattered the quiet.

My eyes flew open. Someone or something was outside. I jumped from the bed to peer out the window.

"Oh my God, it's some kind of animal."

Something small and round was walking towards the backyard.

I closed the window and locked it, then ran back to bed and jerked the sheet up to my neck. I was so scared. What if it got in the house?

After a minute or two, sweat covered my body again. I kicked my legs up and down with enough force to tug the sheet off me.

"Gee," I growled aloud. "Will, I ever get any sleep?" I laughed at myself. I could just imagine the five o'clock news headline: Stranger dies in bed on the first night in her new house because of the Louisiana heat.

As I was finally dozing again, I heard what sounded like footsteps upstairs.

"This can't be happening," I grumbled, exhausted to the point of killing whatever was making noise.

I pulled the lamp closer, lit the wick, and headed upstairs in my bare feet and nightshirt. What started out as anger slowly subsided with each step until it was replaced with a gripping fear of the unknown. I hadn't taken time to investigate the upstairs, so I felt as if I was wandering into uncharted territory.

Every bad scenario came to my mind. Maybe there was another animal up there, or maybe someone broke in. Well, hell, they didn't have to break-in. They could have walked in through the front door since I didn't lock it when I went to the store.

Maybe someone was living up there. I should have checked the house thoroughly before I went to bed. I'd heard stories about people finding strangers living in their attic who only moved about at night, rummaging through the cabinets for food.

I tiptoed, carefully searching each bedroom to find dust and dirt and another broken window. The first thing on my morning list was to board up the window as I did the one downstairs, and then try to find someone to fix all the other stuff.

Each door and window received a thorough inspection. Everything was locked, just as I'd left it. I grabbed a knife from the kitchen and headed back to my room, confident I had done all I could to protect myself.

After placing the knife under my pillow, I was feeling more empowered, knowing I had protection. With that thought, I drifted off to sleep.

◈

The sheers tickled my face, waking me from my deep needed sleep. The morning sun glimmered, and the gentle breeze was heavenly.

For a minute, I was disoriented. Something wasn't right. Why was the curtain in my face? Had it somehow made its way from beside the bed to above the brass headboard?

I jumped from the mattress. Someone had moved my bed with me in it. When I'd laid down last night, the window had been on the right side, instead of behind the headboard.

I backed away from the window, with my heart racing. Something cold and wet stopped me. I looked down, shocked to find a puddle of water. Wet footprints left a path out of the room. The trail led me halfway down the hall where they disappeared in front of the closet.

A gust of wind ruffled my hair, and I lifted my head, my eyes zoning in on the wide-open front door.

My hand went to my heart. Oh no, someone broke in last night.

"Miss Sarah? You okay?"

That was all I heard before my body hit the floor. Next thing I remembered, someone lifted me and set me in my old recliner.

"I'll get you some water." The familiar voice faded for a moment. "Miss Sarah, are you all right?"

My eyes opened to Brian Thibodeaux holding bottled water in one hand and patting my cheek with the other.

"Here, drink this," Brian insisted as he removed the top and handed it to me.

I took a sip, careful not to choke.

"What happened?" My voice was as weak as I felt.

"I'm sorry. I think I scared you. I came to check on you and to bring you the second set of keys I found, and when I got to the door, you turned pale and just fainted in front of me."

What about seeing him at the door had scared me?

"Oh, yeah, I remember now."

I jumped up, almost falling, and Brian reached out to steady me. I ran to the front door to check the lock. Everything looked fine. The bedroom was my next stop. The water was gone, and the bed was where it was supposed to be.

My head was fuzzy as I made my way back to the living room. Maybe I'd dreamed it all since I'd had a terrible time getting to sleep.

"Brian, did you open the front door?" After all, he'd brought me a second set of keys.

"No, it was already open."

"I locked that door last night. I know I did."

Brian laughed. "You know these old houses. They have their own personality. What I mean is, sometimes the door doesn't catch, and even if you lock it, it'll still open. Or maybe the wind blew it open."

"Yes, you may be right."

Why was Brian acting so nonchalant? There was no breeze strong enough last night to even move a set of chimes on the front porch, much less a heavy door.

I felt uncomfortable as Brian leered at my legs instead of my eyes. At that moment, I realized I was standing in the living room in my short nightgown.

"Excuse me a minute." Turning several shades of red, I ran to my bedroom, dressed, and then rejoined my company.

"You said something about keys."

"Yes, I have an extra set," he said as he handed them to me. "You don't look like you had a good first night at your house."

"It was unbearable. It was hot, and in the middle of the night, an animal was outside my window making noise."

Brian laughed. "I would suggest you get some traps. I see you have an armadillo making holes in your yard."

"Oh, that's what I saw last night." It relieved me that at least I knew part of the mystery.

"Well, I've taken up enough of your time," Brian said as he headed towards the door. "I'd get someone to check this door out if I were you and get you some traps."

"Yeah, sure, I'll do that."

With a wave, he was out the door.

I waited until the sound of the car was gone, to investigate the door again. There was no evidence anyone had tampered with it. I closed and locked the door twice, and it worked fine. I pulled, pushed, and jumped on the floor inside the door and out on the porch. The lock was solid.

My mind was muddled with thoughts.

The only conclusion I could believe was that someone else had a key.

Maybe it was Brian. After all, he'd had a second set.

Did he move my bed while I was sleeping, but what would be the point?

I didn't know what, but something was not right with that man.

A terrible chill went through me.

CHAPTER 6

*B*rian was right. I needed a carpenter slash wild animal remover.

In less than five minutes, I was in the car and headed to town. I figured if the hardware store didn't know someone who could help, they could give me advice on how to paint, and I could just do it myself.

The thought of messing up my hair and nails made my skin crawl, but a girl had to do what a girl had to do. Plus, I had rubber gloves. If only there was a rubber suit, I could buy.

I turned left onto Highway One and realized I was driving in the wrong direction when I passed the Walmart from the day before. When I tried finding a place to turn around, I ended up in the parking lot of a hardware store.

What luck! I couldn't have planned it better if I'd tried.

I made a mental note of the things I needed to have fixed and tried putting my list in order of importance.

The sun was so hot; it was hard to breathe. I wondered if it was closer to the Earth in Louisiana than in New York. Perspiration was beading on my skin by the time I walked four steps. I giggled as I visualized me as a red Popsicle, melting with each step, leaving a sticky, red, wet footprint behind me, and just as I reached the door, I turned into a puddle of melted mess.

The air conditioning hit my body with a blast of arctic air as soon as I stepped inside. I stood for a moment with my eyes closed and a smile on my face, enjoying the kiss of cool air on my skin, thankful I made it without melting.

"Can I help you?" the cashier asked.

I opened my eyes to find a short, plump, older woman about fifty-years-old with short curled brown hair, which was graying by her temples. She smiled at me, and I looked at her nametag.

"Yes, Mary, I just moved here, and I was hoping you could recommend a carpenter."

"Where're you living, hun?"

I explained the general direction of my house.

She eyed me for a minute as if she was trying to place who I was.

"Pauline Bordelon's old place?"

"Yes, how did you know?" I asked, astonished.

"There's not too much around here I don't know." She giggled with a wink. "Plus, it's the only house on that road that's been vacant for a while. Pauvre bête. I knew Pauline. She was . . . nice." Mary hesitated.

Mary didn't have to tell me what she was thinking because I saw it on her face. Yes, I knew my aunt was strange, but at least Mary got to meet her.

"You'll be needing someone local." She smiled. I could see the wheels turning in her head as she thought for a moment. "You know, Jessie used to work for Miss Pauline. You should ask him to help. He probably knows that house better than anyone."

"Great, do you have his phone number?" I asked as I searched my purse for a pen and paper.

She laughed. "Mais, he ain't got no phone, Boo. You need to go out to your backyard there and take that old pirogue over to the other side of Spring Bayou, and that's where he'll be."

"Uh, sure, okay." I turned to walk out the door, more confused than when I'd gone in.

As I drove home with no supplies, I wondered if I needed to stop somewhere and buy a translation book. The people there sure talked funny, and what in the world was a pirogue?

Pulling up the driveway, I couldn't believe my eyes. That damn front door was open again.

"What the hell? Did I forget to lock it again?" I slammed my car door and stomped up the steps. I was really getting aggravated. "This is bullshit!" I said loudly as I did a quick search again through the house to make sure everything was in order.

Nothing seemed to be disturbed, so I crossed the

room to the only bookshelf in my aunt's house and searched for a dictionary. Lucky for me she had one. First, I searched for P, then Pe. No, nothing there. Then I searched Pi. There it was.

Pirogue: A dugout; any boat resembling a canoe.

"A boat? Why in the hell didn't she just say a boat?"

Still mad about the door, I stomped out to the boat dock as if I was killing roaches under my feet. I stopped at the edge of the water where the dock began.

Something was different. I eyed the dock for several minutes and realized the boat from the day before was gone.

"Someone's using my dock." I declared aloud. I wondered if it was the same person who was breaking into my house. I looked left and then right. I didn't see one of those pirogues anywhere. "Maybe that weird, canoe type boat is over there," I whispered.

Being careful of wildlife and insects, I searched the weeds and tall grass from the dock to a small clearing about twenty feet away. Several feet into the over-growth, I found it. Inching my way closer and closer to the odd-looking boat, I noticed how small it was. I could not believe my eyes. Who in their right mind would get in a toy boat? Well, the dictionary was right. It was defi-nitely shaped like a canoe. The way it was made, made me think it would be very unsteady.

"I can do this," I said as I steadied myself enough to put one foot in the boat. Then something cold and wet hit my wrist. I lifted my arm to find a tiny green frog latched onto me. I let out a shriek of fear and disgust.

"Oh my god, oh my god!" I screamed louder and louder.

I flung my arm, losing my balance, and falling on my butt half in and half out of the shallow water by the bank. I squirmed until I was sure that gross, cold, slimy thing was off me.

The foot in the water slid further and further away from the bank, causing me to sink even deeper in the muddy water of the bayou. My legs split like an Olympic gymnast.

Tiny green specks of dirt and algae floated on the water's surface, which had me gagging uncontrollably. I was more determined than ever to get out of the muck and mire, so I flipped over and crawled forward on my hands and knees. Finally, I was making progress.

When I was far enough from the water's edge, I looked back at the path I'd cut through the weeds. My mud-streaked clothes made me angry, and tears poured down my face. Never had I been so dirty in all my life. I was so thankful I'd worn none of my good clothes but had found some older clothes at the bottom of my suitcase.

Anger built up in me as I pondered my predicament, replacing the tears.

"If you think you're going to get the best of me, you have another thing coming," I growled at my circumstance.

My fists tightened by my side. Feeling like I was losing the fight with nature was both overwhelming and frustrating. I huffed under my breath as I swiped at the mud with a soggy tissue from my pocket.

"You may win the fight, but I swear I'll win the war," I yelled as I balanced on a log, and with a careful step, got in the pirogue.

Steadying myself, I sat down with a sigh of triumph, took the oar, and pushed away from the shore, heading across the bayou as Mary had said to do. Even though it was very unsteady, and I felt like I could tip over at any minute, I felt a sense of accomplishment.

The sun was high in the sky, and it was so hot, perspiration was burning my eyes as it ran down my face. The water was calm and eerie. I saw things splashing and bubbles rising to the surface and wondered if I'd bitten off more than I could chew.

Centering myself, I took the paddle and made slow, careful strokes to the opposite side of the bayou. I edged beneath the overhanging trees to get out of the sun, finding it was just a tad cooler in the shade. I looked back and realized just how far I was from my old rickety dock.

"I can do this! I can do this! I can do this," I pleadingly told myself.

The vegetation seemed even thicker on that side the bayou. I peered around at everything. My eyes bulged in fear and dread of some wild animal jumping out of the thicket or water and attacking me. That grotesque frog had been more than enough to deal with.

Around the bend was another dock. It stood about seven feet high above the water and about thirty feet long, stopping at a small hill. That must be it. I concentrated so hard to steady the boat as I navigated that I didn't look up until I hit a post. I felt as embarrassed as I had the day before when I'd run into the tree in the backyard.

A small white rope dangled from a ladder, so I carefully tied the boat and tried steadying myself to climb out of the pirogue.

Gripping one side rail of the ladder with caution, I pulled myself up, hugging it as if my life depended on it. Steadying myself while the pirogue moved away from the dock was difficult. As soon as I thought it was safe, I positioned my feet on the bottom step of the ladder and worked my way to the top. Climbing onto the dock was a huge victory for me.

Until I looked up and saw a man standing inches from me. Startled, I jerked back, propelling my body over the water. Strong arms grabbed me around my waist, saving me from taking another bath in the swamp. I gazed into the most gorgeous hazel eyes I had ever seen.

"Watch out, pretty lady. You almost did a backflip into the bayou." He eyed me and then laughed. "It kind of looks like you could use a good dip, though."

He was holding me so firm; I felt like I was against a brick wall. The stranger made me think of a Greek God with his chiseled facial features. His red lips were perfectly formed, captivating me to the point of wanting him to kiss me from to the moon and back.

"Are you all right, miss?"

I cleared my throat and tried to push away from him.

"Hold on. If I release my grip, you'll fall. Move towards me the best you can, away from the edge."

"My God, I'm almost in your pocket now. How do you expect me to move closer?"

His grip tightened around my waist with my face pressed against his chest. Oh my, he smelled so good, so clean, so refreshing. He lifted me off the edge of the dock, and turning from his waist, lowered me until my feet touched solid ground again.

My breath caught in my chest, and blood rushed throughout my body so fast, I fell limp against him. Deep down inside, I didn't want him ever to release me. The chemistry between us was stronger than anything I'd ever felt. I looked in his hazel eyes again and realized he was watching me more intently than before.

His arms loosened until I was standing on my own. I swayed under his hypnotic stare, and his hands grabbed my arms to steady me again.

"Are you okay?"

I heard his soft question, but I couldn't speak.

"Miss, are you okay?"

After a second or two, I found my voice. "Yes, of course."

"So, what's a pretty little city girl like you doing out here in the swamps?"

"I, uh, I was looking for someone." For the life of me, I couldn't remember who though.

All I could do was gaze at the awesome specimen of a man and admire every inch of him. From his dark-brown hair, partly covering his face, all the way down a body that looked like he spent every waking moment in the gym. His skin was tanned by the sun and had the slightest glisten from perspiration. I lost myself in his hazel eyes and realized he must be at least five-foot-nine or maybe even eleven. The hunk of a man was wearing old overalls with the top half hanging by his waist, exposing every inch of his muscled chest.

"Hello? Miss, who are you looking for?"

"Jessie," I whispered, spellbound by his eyes.

He laughed. "You found him."

CHAPTER 7

*D*amn, he was Jessie? Well, there might be something worth staying around Lousy-Ana for, after all. My face flushed six shades of red.

"Hi Jessie, my name is Sarah Hamilton. I moved into the Bordelon house across the bayou from you." I extended my hand, but thought twice about shaking his, considering the chemistry I felt being near him.

My logical mind turned inside out, wondering why my pulse was up and my heartbeat was racing. Sarah would never lose control with a man, not even Hank, and especially with someone who dressed like a bum. How could I be attracted to someone like him? He'd probably never left the swamps before or finished school.

The stranger didn't have an accent like everyone else I'd met, so I wondered if he was a transplant like me.

"It's boiling out here. Would you like to come up to the house for something cold to drink?" Jessie asked with a twinkle in his eyes, snapping me back to the present.

Yes, thank you." We walked up the steps to a well-kept house. I had to ask. "Are you from here? You don't seem to have an accent."

He smiled, and my heart beat fast again. He was already handsome, but his smile showed perfect white teeth that seemed to take his flawless ten face to the highest number imaginable. I'd seen good-looking men before but never had the hair on my arms and neck stood up around them.

"I'm from here. In fact, this old house was my mom and dads. They built it when they first married and passed it down to me." He pointed to a rocker on the front porch. "Have a seat."

While I was sitting, he walked into the house, and a short time later, returned with iced tea.

He sat beside me, took a sip, and kicked his feet up on the front porch railing. "As far as my accent, I went off to college and found I didn't get as many stares if I dropped some Cajun slang from here."

"You-- you went to college? What did you study?"

"You look surprised, Sarah," Jessie said with a mischievous grin. "I mainly studied business." He set his glass down and stared at me. "When I first went off to college, I wanted a ticket out of the swamps. Wanted to make a name for myself in the marketing world. You know, the business suit, tie, and the whole nine yards. But, as the years went by, and I watched my parents' health decline, I realized—" he paused for a minute, "—

there just isn't any place like home. So, I came back."
Jessie repositioned himself on the rocker and stared out
over the bayou. "I'm perfectly happy here doing odd jobs
and living a simple life. You look at things a little differently when you have family struggles to overcome."

This last sentence seemed to make him somber, so I
decided to reroute our conversation.

"Well, Jessie, the reason I'm here is I need some work
done at my place, and I was told you used to work for
my Aunt Pauline."

He looked at me with both eyebrows lifted. "Yes, I
did. So, you inherited the old house?" Jessie asked.

"As a matter of fact, I did."

After a minute, Jessie replied, "I'd be happy to help
you out. I've worked there a time or two. I'm very
surprised to know that Pauline had an heir. She never
had any company or mentioned anyone."

"Well, to be honest, I didn't know I had an Aunt until
I was notified by a lawyer in town."

We sat there, looking out over the water in silence
for a couple of minutes as I waited for the next move.

Jessie took several gulps of tea, set it down, and said,
"Come on, I'll bring you home in my boat and tow the
pirogue back for you. Pirogues aren't the easiest way of
transportation."

I laughed, looking down at myself. "You got that
right."

On the trip back, I watched Jessie as he maneuvered
his boat and realized I'd misjudged him. He might
appear to be a bum from the swamps, but with his good

looks and college education, he would make it in New York with no problems.

He cut the motor on his flat-bottom boat and let it glide right next to the dock with such ease as if he had done it a thousand times before.

After walking off the dock, I turned and pointed at the warped, scarred wood. "Here's a small project for you to do."

"I'm sorry about that. I really should have fixed this a long time ago, since I use it all the time," Jessie said.

I stared at the boat and the way he'd tied it off and realized; it was the boat that was here the other day. Maybe he was the one who came into the house. He said he knew the place. It was possible he had a key. Well, I was going to fix that soon enough.

As we walked around the house, he pointed out little problems. "Do you want your house painted?"

"Yes, of course. Right now, I'm more concerned with the broken windows and the locks on the doors. Oh, and the wild animals around here."

"Wild animals?" he asked with his eyes widened.

"Yes, I believe I have an armadillo that we need to get rid of."

"You really are a city girl, aren't you?" he asked with a mischievous grin.

"What's that got to do with anything?" I huffed.

"Well, I don't mean to be disrespectful, but you live in the woods, practically surrounded by swamp water, and you think you have an armadillo? Lady, you got more than just armadillos out here." He ran his hand through his hair, pulled a cap from his back pocket, and placed it on his head. "I can trap armadillos every day and twice on Sunday, and you'll never be rid of them or any of the other animals that are more dangerous than that out here. It's best to be in harmony with your surroundings than to fight against nature, who, by the way, always wins."

Feeling as if I didn't really know enough about nature to argue with him, I decided to agree. I nodded.

We made our way to the front porch where I told him I wanted to change the locks on the front and back door.

I watched his expression, and he seemed perfectly fine with the idea.

"So, would you like me to get started today?"

"Yes, if that's all right." Relief that he'd agreed to help flooded me.

"Ok, well, it's getting late, and we need to get some supplies from the hardware store."

"Great, I'll get my purse."

He took a nicely folded tee shirt out of one of the deep pockets on his overalls. I stared as he put his cap between his knees, pulled his tee shirt over his head, and tugged the front of his overalls up around his shoulders. I realized the world was standing still, and so was I. I didn't mean to ogle him, but damn, he looked good.

The girls in the office where I'd worked had a fire-fighter's calendar with men that looked just like him. Boy, would they be jealous if they saw me up close and personal with Mr. Man.

I started to giggle as I walked away, thinking of how those women would drool over Jessie. I'd be the envy of the office.

Even though the front door was closed, when I entered the house, something just didn't feel right. I reached for my purse on the side table and realized it wasn't there. My car keys were there, but my purse was missing.

Did I leave it on my bed or somewhere else?

I rushed to my bedroom to find my bed moved again. I stepped back and did a slow one-eighty to see if anything else was off. That's when I saw an image on the closet mirror and jumped. It was me, but it didn't look like me. A very dirty, disheveled woman stared back from the mirror. My God, I had dried gunk all over my pants and splatters on my shirt. My face was smeared with so much mud; I didn't recognize my own reflection.

"I don't have time for this crap," I said in exasperation.

Being an overly OCD, neat freak, I couldn't help but change my clothes, wash my face, and brush my hair. There was no time for a shower since I had Mr. Man waiting outside. The thought of a stranger at my house didn't faze me like the dirt on my face. I put the trip to the hardware store on hold, because, to me, it was more important to look good than to go buy supplies.

I ran from room to room looking for my purse until I found it on the kitchen table. A startled gasp slipped from my lips. There was no way I'd left it there. Scared, I clutched my purse close to my chest and ran out the front door, right into Jessie's chest.

He grabbed me. "Whoa there, little lady, there's no reason to rush. The hardware store isn't going anywhere."

His smile faded as he looked at my face then gently pushed me against the open door. As he studied the expression on my face, I knew he saw my fear and felt my body shaking. He wasted no time walking into my house and looking around.

My head down and fear gripping me, I heard Jessie walking around and opening every door in the house.

Out of the corner of my eye, I saw something. I tilted my head to the side. In the hallway by the closet door, a shimmering mist turned, forming into something.

"What the hell is that?" I whispered in a shaky voice.

CHAPTER 8

*T*he thick vapor grew in size and shape. As it turned and swirled, it took on all the colors of the rainbow. Mesmerized, I watched as it dissipated. What stood before me was a woman, staring at me.

I gasped, stepping against the doorframe, and reaching behind me for support. Her light blue full-length gown had a darker blue lace overlay. It sparkled like a typical New York City night. Her long, white hair cascaded down the left side of her body, stopping at her waist. It was like looking at an older version of myself.

Nothing came out when I gulped and tried to yell for Jessie.

The woman melted away into a light haze, and then nothing.

She didn't have that glow about her like the angel in my condo bathroom. She seemed real for a second until she disappeared before my eyes.

"Hello, Earth to Sarah," Jessie said, trying to get my attention.

I looked at him, wondering where he'd come from.

"You look like you saw a ghost," Jessie said with concern on his face.

If my back had not been propped against the door-frame, and my hands gripping the side, I would have fallen to the floor.

"Do you need to sit down?" he asked as he led me to a chair in the living room without waiting for my reply.

My body was weak, and I found myself sitting down on the antique chair, then questioning how I got there. Last I remembered, I was standing at the door.

"Okay, are you going to tell me what's going on?" Jessie asked.

"I couldn't find my purse. I always leave it on the side table by the door." I pointed in the general direction. "When I went to look for it in the bedroom, I noticed that my bed had been moved, just like last night. Then I changed my clothes and continued to look for my purse. I found it in the kitchen on the table." Inhaling deeply, I gripped the edge of the chair. "I have never left my purse there before. I-- I got scared and ran into you. Then I saw, I saw, I presume, my Aunt Pauline." I paused. "She stood right there, in the hallway." I tried to swallow and get my thoughts in order. "She had long white hair pulled to the side, and she was wearing a sparkling, lacey dress with a high neck, and... And She looked like me, only older."

Jessie kneeled down in front of me and asked. "You said you never saw your aunt before, right?"

"Right. Why?"

"Have you seen any pictures of her?"

"No, why?"

"I don't know what to make of all this, but your aunt had long white hair, and I remember her having a blue lace dress she would wear occasionally. She kept her hair up in one of those buns." He circled the top of his head with his hand. Jessie sat back on the heel of his feet. "Sarah, I don't know what to tell you to ease your fear, but I don't think your Aunt Pauline is here to hurt you." Jessie pulled his cap off and ran his fingers through his thick, dark, wavy hair and repositioned the cap again. "I know we're strangers, Sarah, but I have to tell you this. From time to time, I see my parents standing on the dock, holding each other at sunset. They both passed away just months from each other. It could be my imagination because I desperately miss them and want to see them. I'm not sure if it's real or not real. I really don't know, and I don't care. I presume they come to visit, or it's just a message of love, or maybe they never left. I try not to analyze it. I just enjoy seeing them together, happy and just as in love as ever."

My mind was so confused. First, I saw angels, and now I saw my dead aunt. Then I moved next to someone who saw his dead parents. What was going on?

Jessie hung his head momentarily, then looked deep into my eyes, "I don't know why your bed was moved or why your purse wasn't where you left it, but I didn't see anyone here. Do you want me to call the cops?

I wasn't sure why I didn't tell Jessie about the puddle, or the footprints, or even the condo angels I saw in New York. Jessie seemed nice, but something inside me screamed at me to trust no one. I was desperate to defuse the situation. My habit was to push uncomfortable situations out of my mind 'til I could get a better grip on it. If I didn't, I'd get overwhelmed to the point of crying and hysteria, and I wasn't in the mood for crying in front of the handsome stranger, plus it would mess up my fresh makeup.

"No, there's no need to get the cops out here. Like you said you saw nothing. We can't sit here all day trying to analyze everything, so I say, let's go to the store." I smiled, changing the subject. I had to leave the house and catch my breath.

As we drove to the store, I told myself there was no way I would let this go. Whether someone haunted my new house, or someone was playing a dirty joke on me, I would find the underlying cause if it was the last thing I did.

We fit everything we needed in one shopping cart. As we rolled up to the front counter next to the register, I realized I was starving and grabbed a Slim Jim for some protein.

Jessie replaced my Slim Jim with a granola bar with nuts and seeds.

I looked at him as if he was crazy. He laughed.

"You may be from the city, but you don't know what's good for you."

"Yeah, okay, country boy, whatever you say," I said sarcastically, my eyes squinting at him.

"Well hey, sweetie, back so soon?" Mary said as she hurried up front to ring us up. "I'm sorry to make you wait," she said as she eyed Jessie. "I see you took my advice and found Jessie to help you around that old house."

"I did, thank you."

"How are you doing, Jessie?" Mary asked as she rang up each item.

"I'm doing just fine, Miss Mary. I guess I have you to thank for this job?"

"Well, hun, you know it. You did such a good job on my porch last year that I just had to spread the word."

Jessie grinned and grabbed our items as I paid.

"Y'all come again."

When we exited the hardware store, Jessie chuckled. "Spread the word? That woman knows everybody's business from here to Baton Rouge. She'll spread the word all right." After a moment, he said, "But at least she has gotten me some business." Jessie took the keys from my hand and loaded the car. "Get in, sweetheart. I'm driving."

I was tickled at how he called me sweetheart and just took control. It was a good feeling inside as if I didn't have to carry the load of the last couple of days alone.

"I can't remember if anyone has ever called me sweetheart or hun before." I smiled.

"Get used to it. People around here will call their enemies honey, sugar, boo, and babe, just to name a few. It's just the way we talk."

Jessie turned left when he should have gone right. For a split second, I got scared. What was he doing? Jessie looked over at me and saw the fear on my face as I gripped my purse until my knuckles turned white.

"Hold up there, don't go getting paranoid. I'm just taking you to see some sights. After your scare this morning, you need something to take your mind off things."

He was right about that. I eased the grip on my purse and calmed down.

"I-- I--"

"Don't worry about it, sweet thing. I know what city folks are like. I can only imagine what it's like in New York. From now on, I promise I'll tell you what I'm doing first before I take it upon myself to just kidnap you like this again. Deal?"

"Deal. How'd you know I was from New York?"

"Your accent is undeniably from New York. I had a friend in college with the same accent."

Jessie drove down and around the narrow roads, giving me a glimpse of other houses in the area and teaching me a little in the process. The camps on Spring Bayou were, for the most part, simply made homes. A lot of the structures were built ten feet off the ground, or more, in case of flooding. Though some people lived in them full time, others were used as weekend get-aways.

As Jessie drove, he explained how Spring Bayou behind my house stretched beyond several cities, and the woods were so large, they reached the Great Mississippi River and stretched into another state.

Jessie seemed to live and breathe his woodsy environment, but holy cow, of all the places in the world to be stuck, mine had to be some place in the middle of Nature Valley, USA. My stomach turned at the thought, knowing it went on forever. All I longed for was getting my nails done, or even better, a hot rock massage with essential oils, in a quiet, dimly lit room with soft music playing in the background.

"Hello, Earth to Sarah." Jessie's amused voice broke through my spa fantasy. "Come in with me while I pick up some things."

We were at a small grocery store in a small town, and Jessie was holding the car door open for me. How long had I been stuck in my brain?

When we walked in the door, a wonderful aroma of food hit me. Jessie turned to the right, but I followed my nose to the back of the store. There was a display of meats, but it smelled like cooked food.

The man at the counter asked if I wanted some fresh cracklings.

"Some what?" I asked.

"Or maybe I can interest you in some fresh boudin?"

"I'm sorry, sir, but I'm not from around here. I don't know what those foods are, but something sure smells good."

The man grabbed a small, thin piece of white paper

and used it to wrap something bubbly and tan. "Here, try this crackling."

I sank my teeth into a salty piece of heaven. Oh my, it was good.

About that time, Jessie came up and nudged my arm. "I can't leave you alone for a minute, and you're putting something bad in your mouth."

"You've got to be kidding. This is awesome," I said as I took another nibble.

"I'm not talking about how it tastes. I know how good it is, but do you know what you're eating?"

As I swallowed the last crunchy morsel, I grinned at him and shrugged.

Jessie led me to the front to purchase his items while I searched the paper for more crumbs. As we exited the building, I was tempted to run back inside to get another crackling.

"Do you know what you just ate? What you ate will probably clog your arteries before we get back to Marksville. It's pig fat and skin." Jessie opened the car door for me, then walked around the car and got inside

"Pig fat and skin?" I asked, licking my lips to get the flavor of salt and cracklings. Then a picture of a slab of fat and skin popped in my mind, and I shivered. "Gross. I ate pig fat? Gross, gross, gross."

"Listen up, here. Cajun people are used to living off the land and not wasting any part of any animal. These people went through hard times, and they learned to eat anything and everything. This is generational eating. They pass their recipes from one generation to another.

They can make a damn possum taste like elegant cuisine. So next time, before you put something in your mouth, ask me. Understand?"

Stunned silent, all I could do was nod. Oh my god, what kind of people were these?

When we got back, Jessie carried the hardware supplies to the porch and made himself at home by putting everything away. It was obvious it wasn't his first time working at the house.

He walked to the corner of the house, turned on the outside water faucet, and drank from it. I know my eyes were bugging out of my head as I watched this man drink ordinary tap water. Oh my, he drank directly out of the facet, no filter or anything.

He looked at me and laughed. He shook his head side-to-side. "I have so much to teach you, city girl."

"My name is Sarah," I demanded, perturbed by his rude comment.

"Don't get mad, boo. I understand your kind, better than you know."

"My kind?" I yelled a little louder than I should have. Blood rushed to my face, burning my cheeks.

"Okay, I keep putting my foot in my mouth. It's really late, how about I head home, and we start fresh in the morning?"

I nodded, and we said our goodbyes and went our separate ways.

I walked in the house, then ran back to the kitchen window to watch Jessie as he jumped in his boat and started the motor.

I wondered where the day went. It seemed like only hours ago since my day started.

The sun was hanging low in the sky, spreading a thick orange and gold mixture of color with a slight pink outline. As the boat left the dock, I walked out the back door onto the porch and wondered if I had ever seen a beautiful sky in the city before. It pained me to admit that the reflection on the water with the backdrop of greenery was breathtaking.

CHAPTER 9

The night was sticky hot, but at least the electricity was on. A fan sat in front of the open window to keep me cooler than the night before. As soon as the important things were fixed on the house, I would start saving money for central air. With the heat and humidity in Louisiana, it was hard to imagine not having it. Was Aunt Pauline that tight with money?

After tossing and turning for a while, I finally fell into a deep sleep sometime past midnight.

In my dream, I was in Aunt Pauline's unsteady pirogue. The choppy water was splashing in and rocking it back and forth. Something squeaked loud enough to pull me from my sleep, and at that moment, I realized I was literally moving.

My bed was sliding across the floor. Startled, I jerked up and saw a dark figure at the end of my bed. I screamed with every ounce of my being. The intruder seemed surprised, then turned and ran out of my room. As fast as I could I throw the sheet off, bare feet and all, I ran after the dark figure in time to see him exit my front door, leaving it wide open.

As fast as possible, I followed the figure down the steps. At the bottom, I paused, wondering which way to go. It was so dark and scary, and the thought of wild animals left me paralyzed and suspended in time as fear gripped me.

Forced to make a quick decision, I ran around to the back of the house. I saw nothing. It was as if he'd disappeared. Maybe I'd wasted too much time paralyzed in fear. I listened intently but heard only the slight rustle of the leaves, some damn crickets chirping, and frogs hollering out for attention.

"Where the hell is that son-of-a-bitch?" I asked as I tried to regain my composure.

Exhausted from lack of sleep and all the hoorah since moving into the house, I longed for my bed in New York, and the feeling of safety in my high-rise, air-conditioned condominium. I didn't know what was going on, but I would be glad when Jessie came to change my locks in a couple of hours.

Too shaken up, I couldn't go back to sleep. So, after rechecking the doors and windows, I grabbed a bottled water and sat in the living room. Staring off into space grew old quickly, so I checked out Aunt Pauline's books and grabbed the first one that caught my attention.

Reading always made me sleepy. I curled up in my old recliner and read about a young tomboy living near the swamps. Her dad came back from the dead to talk to her. That chick was tough. Her circumstances were quite similar to mine, but I wasn't near as brave. Too bad it was fiction. I sure would like to get help from her or one of the other strong-willed characters. I giggled.

A couple of hours later with the sun peering through the windows, I smiled and closed the book.

"I love happy endings."

I hoped my situation ended up just as good as the main character in the book. I looked at the title, *Louisiana Cajun Girl.* That's what I needed to become to deal with the problem directly and run my intruder out of town.

Who was I kidding? I wasn't born in Louisiana. I didn't hunt and fish like that girl. It was hopeless. I was a city girl, lost in the muck and mire of the swamps. Bayou living was a completely new ball game. This place would literally eat me alive if I wasn't careful, and that was just the backyard.

Feeling defeated before the day began, I dressed and made coffee. As I was sipping my first cup at the kitchen table, I heard footsteps and a knock. Almost spilling my coffee, I ran to open the back door. Expecting to find nothing again, I was surprised to see Jessie.

"Thank God, you're here," I said, falling into his arms.

"Hey there, what's crawled up your britches so early in the morning?"

"Oh my, what a terrible night I had. I'm not sure if I should call the police or what."

"Hold on, there. What happened?" Jessie asked with concern on his face.

"There was a stranger in my room last night, and he ran out the front door before I could see his face."

"What?" Jessie's jaw tightened as he gently pushed me back and headed straight down the hall. I followed him as he searched through the rooms. "So, you say he went out the front door, then disappeared?"

"Yes."

Jessie squeezed my shoulders, providing a needed comfort. "It's all right, Boo. I'll change your locks right now. Just be thankful you didn't get hurt."

"I am thankful. Actually, I think I scared him. He ran out of here so fast that I didn't see where he went."

"Okay, pretty lady, I need two things from you."

"You name it," I said, eager for his help.

Jessie paused and smiled with his eyebrow lifting. "You better be careful what you say. I could take that, several ways."

"Well, you know what I mean." My cheeks burned, making me wonder how many shades of red my face was.

Jessie laughed. "Okay, on a serious note," he said with a grin and a twinkle in his eyes. "I need to borrow your phone, and I smell coffee. Would you fix me a cup with just a little creamer and a level spoon of sugar?"

I handed him my cell phone. Goosebumps covered me as I headed to the kitchen. Mr. Man had such a way about him. I felt like putty in his hands. If he'd told me to jump off the roof, I would have.

"No, I don't see how they could have gotten in. No, nothing is missing. Sure, I'll be here, Gerald."

He was talking to the Sheriff's Department. I took his mug and left the kitchen, but stopped when I saw a puddle in front of the hallway closet.

"What the hell?"

I grabbed a rag and wiped up the water, then continued to the front porch where Jessie was bent over, digging in his toolbox. When I handed him his coffee, I realized I'd left mine in the kitchen. On my way to get it, I noticed another water puddle in the same spot.

No matter how hard I searched, I couldn't figure out where the water was coming from. I went back to the kitchen for my coffee and another rag and returned to see the spot was dry.

"This is crazy," I whispered under my breath. Without hesitation, I rushed to see if maybe Jessie had cleaned up the floor. I was only gone a second or two. I would have seen him.

He was sitting on the porch, wearing his utility belt, and drinking his coffee. "What's up? You seem distracted."

"No, no, I was just wondering if your coffee was all right?"

Why couldn't I tell Jessie about the times I found water on the floor? I didn't know if maybe, I was hallucinating because of lack of sleep, or if someone was trying to get my attention, considering the condo angels and the woman appearing in the hallway. Plus, could you hallucinate cold water you could feel?

"Well, for a city girl, you did all right. The coffee is strong, just like I like it." Jessie's smile brought me back to the present.

"After last night, I needed it strong," I replied.

It wasn't long before a sheriff's car parked in front of the porch.

Jessie met the man at the bottom of the steps and shook his hand.

"It's good to see you, Jessie," the man said.

"Same here, Gerald. Come, I'd like to introduce you to Sarah Hamilton, the new owner."

An older man about my height stood before me. Soft laugh lines bracketed his sky-blue eyes, deepening when he smiled. His face looked like he had seen more than his fair share of crime.

"Nice to meet you, ma'am. I'm Gerald Juneau. So, you had someone in your house last night?"

"Yes, sir. Around three this morning. I woke up to a dark figure at the end of my bed. He was moving my bed to the side." I knew it sounded strange, but he was real. It's not as if the bed was moving by itself.

"Can you show me where this happened?"

"Yes, follow me."

As we walked to the bedroom, I eyed the spot in front of the closet and was thankful I saw nothing.

Gerald examined the wooden floor in my room and found scratches. "Do you know if the intruder ran out an open front door or a closed one? Did he have to stop to unlock it?"

"No, it was open."

We went back to the front door, and he inspected the lock on the door.

"Doesn't look like someone broke in. Does anyone else have a set of your keys?"

After considering his question for a minute, I said, "Well, Brian Thibodeaux, the lawyer, came by and gave me a second set yesterday."

The officer made notes in a small flip notepad. He then walked around the house with Jessie, with me following behind them.

The officer stopped and turned towards me. "Where was the last place you saw the intruder?"

"Ah, he was fast. I chased him to the front porch, but I didn't see where he went."

"So, you last saw him on the front porch?"

"Well, technically, I saw him go through the front door, then I lost him."

"One last question. You said you saw a shadow. Was the shadow tall or short, fat or thin? Can you give me something to work with?"

With my head down, my mind relived last night. "He was kind of short and stout."

"Okay, Miss Hamilton, that's about all I need to make my report."

Jessie and Gerald shook hands, and Gerald nodded at me.

"Don't worry, Miss Hamilton. Jessie will keep you safe. He worked for us for a while. He knows his stuff. If you ever need anything, call me."

The dust was still settling after Gerald left when

Jessie reached and squeezed my hand. "I'm changing those locks right now."

While Jessie got busy working around the house, I gathered all the sheets to wash. It felt good to be busy cleaning and straitening. It took my mind off the previous night.

By the end of the day, Jessie had replaced the rotten wood on the dock, nailed the loose boards on the house, installed the door locks, fixed the broken windows, and made sure everything was secure. While he was putting his tools up for the day, I peeked around the open door.

"Jessie, will you stay for some homemade soup?" I asked softly, hoping he would.

He turned from his toolbox and smiled. "That sounds great."

Butterflies swarmed in my stomach. I felt like a teenager on her first date with the head of the football team. I combed my hair, brushed my teeth, and made sure I looked good enough to entertain Mr. Man.

The way he took control of the situation was big, impressive points in my book. He seemed so genuine, smart, handsome, well educated, good looking, down to earth, level-headed, and so damn fine. I smiled at myself for referring to his looks more than once.

We took turns serving our soup from the pot on the stove and settled at the kitchen table. We ate in silence. I was so nervous sitting next to Jessie that my body seemed to shake from within and my heart seemed to race. The feelings churning inside me were unlike any I'd ever felt before. There were no butterflies or nervousness with my husband, Hank. There were no feelings involved only a logical choice.

"You seem distracted, Sarah," Jessie said, laying down his spoon.

"Well, I really haven't slept much the last two nights and…"

Jessie reached over the table and covered my hand with his. The words just caught in my throat as I felt the warmth of his hand on mine.

"I, uh, how's the soup?" I asked while trying to hold back this burning desire inside.

In my mind, I wanted to reach over and grab him in my arms, throw all the dishes on the floor, and have my way with him on the kitchen table. It had been so long since someone had touched me. Hank had slowly withdrawn from me in the last year before he'd left me.

"I'm sorry, Sarah. The soup is excellent." He stood up from the table. "It's late, I should be going. Thank you for dinner."

I got up and walked him out onto the back porch.

Jessie hesitated then turned towards me. "Do you want me to stay the night?"

Damn right, I want you to spend the night, was all I could think as he stood there looking down at me.

"You know, I could sleep on the couch. If it would help you feel safer," Jessie said with concern in his voice.

My voice trembled. "Yes, please? I definitely would feel better if you were here."

After the dishes were washed and Jessie's bed made, we sat on the couch telling stories and laughing about my Aunt Pauline. Jessie leaned over and picked up the book I was reading earlier that morning.

"You know the author of this book is a local around here."

"Really, maybe I'll get her to autograph my copy."

"Maybe," Jessie said as he placed the book on the table.

"Jessie, I'm glad you're staying with me tonight, but I really need to get some sleep," I whispered, yawning then standing to leave.

"I'm happy to help. Just holler out if you need anything." Jessie winked.

I smiled as I walked to my bedroom with a deep desire for a good night's sleep and feeling safe now that Jessie was there to guard me.

CHAPTER 10

I slept so sound knowing someone was there that I didn't hear when Jessie walked into my bedroom.

"Morning, city girl, I brought you some coffee."

Groggy, I sat up and reached for my coffee.

Jessie made himself at home and sat on the side of the bed with his coffee. He eyed me.

"What?" I asked, stretching and yawning. "You can't expect me to look good first thing in the morning," I said, with a frown.

"Well, that's just it. You look . . . good. Refreshed and calm. That little crease you have on your forehead when you're scared or stressed disappeared." He paused. "You're a beautiful woman. I don't mean to be so forward." He smiled, cocking his head to the side. "Considering I'm sitting on your bed, but from the first day I rescued you on the dock, all I've been able to do is think of you," Jessie said as he softly laughed.

"What is it? Why are you laughing?" It disappointed me he would make fun of such a special moment.

"You're not even my type. You're a city girl who doesn't know how to get her hands dirty."

I spurted coffee and laughed, too. He was right.

Trying to catch my breath from such a hearty laugh, I said, "When I first met you, I felt the same way. You're not my type either. I thought you were a backward, non-educated bum with good looks." We both laughed again. "But I'm attracted to you, too."

Jessie gazed at me warmly, and my heart leaped in my chest. He reached over and took my hand in his.

"Well, I'm glad we got that out of the way." Jessie cleared his throat. He released my hand, stood up, and hit my leg. "Get up and get dressed. We have work to do." Jessie walked out of the room with a weird smirk on his face.

What the hell just happened? We confirmed our attraction for each other, and he gets up and leaves the room? Shouldn't he at least give me a kiss to seal the deal?

Then I blew into my cupped hand and smelled my breath. Wow, yes, a good thing he left the room. I got up and dressed and was brushing my hair when he walked back in. He looked at me from top to bottom, raising one eyebrow.

"Don't you have anything else you can wear? I'm putting you to work today."

"This is all I have. I've lived in New York my whole life, and this is what we wear."

He went to the closet where my Aunt Pauline's clothes hung, rummaged in the bottom for shoes, then slid one hanger after another for some clothes he threw on the bed.

"You and your aunt are about the same size, and she used to wear this when she worked in the yard." Jessie walked out the door and said over his shoulder, "Finish your coffee, get dressed, and I'll be waiting for you outside."

The morning was turning out weird, already. I loved our close encounter, and I liked the way he took control, but this was intrusive. Telling me what to wear. Who did he think he was? I grinned, knowing I really wasn't mad, just trying to get used to his ways.

As I stood there with Aunt Pauline's clothes in my hand, Jessie peeked around the corner of my doorway again.

"Oh, and don't put on any make-up. You're too pretty to be trying to impress anyone out here."

I stood there with a small grin on my face, examining myself in the closet door mirror. After I dressed, I walked closer to the full-length mirror to see the girl who stood before me. I couldn't believe it, but I didn't even recognize the reflection.

The woman with the expensive taste in clothes and done up hair and nails was now just a woman. He was right. I didn't need to be wearing my city clothes out here. Looking closer at my face without makeup, I had to admit he was right again. I really was pretty without it. Different but pretty. I felt like I was being introduced to another side of Sarah Hamilton.

I exited the front door with a lightness of heart.

Jessie was on a ladder with his tool belt around his waist. He climbed down when he saw me. "You look fantastic, as pretty as a picture." He kissed my forehead.

I felt all warm inside as if I'd never had a compliment before in my life. Something in me wanted to please Jessie, to get all the compliments because it was one thing I never got growing up. I'd worked so hard to make a name for myself, to be somebody, to get approval from the world. This was different. I wasn't showing my talents, my fancy BMW, my high-priced clothes, or condo. I was only being me, and someone saw me. Someone really saw me for me. Best of all, he seemed to like me like this.

"Watch me and do as I do," Jessie said, interrupting my thoughts. He dipped a paintbrush in the white paint, got the excess off, and brushed the wall. "Now you do it." He handed me the paint and paintbrush. "I'll get the top half, and you get the bottom."

I couldn't believe I was doing manual labor. I was painting a house. Never in my wildest dreams did I ever think I would do anything so menial in my entire life. But there I was, and I was determined to do a good job.

"Don't worry, Sarah. If you get paint on you, just know we can wash it off. Okay?"

I smiled up at Jessie. "Okay." Guess that meant rubber gloves weren't needed.

We worked for hours. I finished an entire section

and felt proud of myself until I saw Jessie had done three times the amount.

Jessie grinned. "You're doing great, Sarah."

Getting such a compliment gave me the energy to keep on painting for a little while longer.

We broke for lunch, and I heated the leftover soup.

As we sat to eat, my life felt complete. I was happy and content. There was no rush, rush, rush, or stress from the work-a-day world. It felt great, a little sore, but great.

"Leave the dishes. We have a lot more to get done before this afternoon."

Leave the dishes! I had never left a dirty sink before. Hank and I ate out most of the time, so naturally, dishes weren't even a second thought in my world. An occasional plate here and there was nothing; plus, I had a dishwasher. My hands never got all wrinkly washing dishes.

The further I walked away from the dirty dishes, the lighter I felt. I was defying my nature one step at a time and enjoying it.

Before I picked up my paintbrush, I walked a few feet into the yard to inspect what we'd done so far. The change between the old and new astonished me. Wow, what a difference a fresh coat of paint made.

Movement in the upstairs window caught my eye. I froze. Was someone in the house?

"Jessie!" I said, pointing toward the second level. "There, there's someone upstairs."

Jessie was off the ladder and running into the house

before I could move from my spot. My knees shook and trembled, threatening to give out on me. Dread weighed me down. I walked into the house just as Jessie came down the stairs.

"What did you see, Sarah?"

"Movement in the upstairs right window. It was as if someone was passing by or backing away when I looked up.

"I don't know what you saw, but there was nothing there."

I felt so stupid. Maybe I'd moved my head too fast and thought I'd seen something.

Jessie grabbed my hand, led me to my painting station, and pulled me to him for a hug. Like the first day, I'd met him, I laid my head on his chest and enjoyed the feel of his safe arms around me.

"You'll have to come up with something better than that to get out of work," Jessie said, leaning back to give me a smile and a wink.

"Yeah, well, it almost worked," I said jokingly.

We labored the rest of the afternoon painting. On several occasions one of us caught the other watching each other instead of working. I didn't know what he was thinking, but my mind was definitely not on painting. I was daydreaming of being in his arms in a Jacuzzi. The warm bubbles would massage my aching muscles while his lips would trail down my neck.

"Okay, little lady, that's enough," Jessie said, startling me.

Where did he come from? Did he know what I was thinking?

"Wash up while I clean and put the paint supplies up."

I was happy to be finished. I couldn't imagine what my hair looked like after such a long day. An extreme burning sensation all but made my arms useless. It hurt so bad; I winced every time I moved. It didn't seem to bother Jessie. Hard work seemed to be second nature to him. Mr. Man had brains and muscle. I admired that in him.

Washing up was the best thing ever. Aunt Pauline's claw-foot tub was the perfect size for me to stretch out and close my eyes. The longer I soaked in the hot sudsy water, the better I felt. Relaxing took some of the soreness out of my body. After a couple of minutes, I realized I had a huge grin on my face, despite my aches and pains. So, what was so special about today that had me smiling?

I'm falling in love with Jessie.

My eyes popped open. Before I knew it, I was giggling like a schoolgirl. How could I be in love with Jessie? I'd only known him for a few short days, but I was happy and content with him. I could imagine him in my life forever. It was as if he fit me like a glove.

Hank was a logical decision between two people striving for the same things in life. With Jessie, there was no striving for anything. It was as natural as breathing. Talking together, working, simply being with him, made everything complete.

By the time I finished with my bath and redressed in more of Aunt Pauline's clothes, Jessie had cleaned and stored the tools, washed up the dirty dishes, and then made himself at home, snacking on cut fruit.

"Come, Boo, and have a little snack with me. I have something I want to show you."

It was good eating something someone else had prepared. My stomach had been rumbling for at least an hour, but I was even more excited to see what was up Jessie's sleeve. He took the plate of fruit and we walked out the back door to the porch swing.

The evening was winding down, and it was so comforting spending the quiet moment with Jessie. There was no place else in the world I wanted to be, not even my condo.

As he threw a piece of cantaloupe in his mouth, he smiled and grabbed my hand.

"Come, Cher, you'll like this."

I grabbed a cluster of grapes and smiled. "Okay, let's go."

CHAPTER 11

*J*essie and I ran down the steps to the dock where he helped me into his boat, and we headed across Spring Bayou to his house.

We had just enough time to climb the pier, run to the steps of his house, and turn around to see the most awesome sight I'd ever seen in person.

The sun was setting, and the beautiful landscape defied description. As I sat on the third lowest step of his house, Jessie moved behind me and wrapped his arms around me. I laid my head against his chest, watching in awe and silence the majesty of God's painting.

Every second, the canvas took on another color, so calming and relaxing. The beauty went on across the sky with blues, pinks, whites, and yellows, and even held a touch of lavender.

While the sun was just visible by minutes, a couple

appeared out of thin air, standing on the end of the dock. The man and woman were facing the sunset in each other's arms, side by side, as though they were part of the landscape.

So, this was what Jessie was talking about. His parents were there as if they had always been.

Oh my, when you thought you understood life, it threw you a curve ball that hit you between the eyes.

"Look, my parents made it today for the sunset." Jessie's whisper barely rippled the quiet.

"I wonder if other places in Louisiana have a story to tell as awesome as this?" I was in complete awe. My god, Louisiana was an eerie, unusual place. Aunt Pauline at my place, and Jessie's parents on the dock at sunset.

After a minute or two, he bent down and whispered in my ear. "Where there is love, miracles happen."

As the last ray of the sun melted behind the trees, so did his parents. It was like they came only for that one moment in time.

Jessie lifted me onto his lap. His arms pulled me close, and he kissed me with an explosion of passion. It was as if the world faded away, and there was just the two of us.

Oh wow, I'd never been kissed like that before, and never had I wanted to throw caution to the wind and give myself to a man.

"I've wanted to kiss you all day." He paused with his forehead against mine. "My God, Sarah you do things to me like no one else." With his lips parted, he moved in for another kiss.

I wrapped my arms around his neck, pulling him close and letting him know I wanted him as much as he wanted me. I longed to have this man be a part of my life in every way.

His kiss was warm and passionate. His pang of hunger met my desire. It made me feel as if my soul was melting into his. When our kiss ended, and he eased back, I saw a tear running down his cheek. He wiped it from his face and smiled.

"I feel like I will burst with joy at any second," Jessie said.

"Thank God! I thought there was something wrong."

Jessie wrapped his arms tight around my waist and jumped up, letting out a yell at the top of his lungs. "I don't know what it is about you, Sarah Hamilton, a.k.a. City Girl, but you make me feel like I'm on Mount Everest, like I can conquer the world."

"Jessie, I feel the same way." My hands cupped his face.

With him cradling me like a baby, he carried me up the stairs onto the porch as if I weighed nothing. He set me down with a kiss on my forehead.

"Stay here while I go get some clothes. You're not spending the night alone in that house until I figure out what is going on."

With that comment, I came back to reality. I let out a sigh of relief. A weight lifted from my soul when he said that. The last thing I wanted was to be alone in that house while there were so many unexplained things happening there.

Jessie's boots clomped through the house for several minutes, and then he exited the front door with an army-green backpack on one shoulder and a flashlight in his hand.

"Let's go, sugar pie."

It was the time of day that scared me to my bones. In the sun's place was a partial moon. Otherwise, the sky was pitch black. The city was always light and always busy. However, the bayou was quiet, dark, and eerie, with occasional movement in the water. It was always the unknown that frightened a person. The thought of what could lurk in the water or on land made me remember going to see a scary movie about Big Foot when I was a teenager. Could there really be things like that in the world?

Fear of something big and menacing made me over-grip the seat of the boat. I was thankful I was not alone.

Jessie tied his boat on the dock and helped me out. As we approached the house, we both looked up at the same time and saw what appeared to be a glow of light in my bedroom window.

"Did you see that?" Jessie asked.

"Someone's in my room," I whispered.

"Stay on the porch while I check this out." Jessie made his way to the back door, laid his backpack down, and flipped on his flashlight as he turned the doorknob.

Frozen in fear, I debated what was scarier: being left outside in the dark with the unknown, or going inside with an intruder. I decided the intruder was safer than the alligators, snakes, and possibly Big Foot. I stayed close to the wall as I tiptoed inside through the kitchen to the hallway. When I reached my bedroom door, the light came on, scaring ten years off my life. My hands flew to my mouth to cover the emerging scream.

Someone appeared in the doorway, and I shrieked. Fear overpowered my reasoning. It was Jessie, who came straight to me and wrapped me safe in his arms.

"It's okay, Cher. It's me." Jessie held me a minute, giving me time to calm myself. "Come look at this."

We walked into my bedroom. My bed had been moved under the window again.

"What is it with my bed?" I asked.

After searching the house, the only thing we found was an open window by the front door, the screen behind one of the porch rockers.

"It's kind of hard to close all the windows with this heat," I said as I pulled my cell phone from my back pocket and handed it to Jessie. "Call your friend, Gerald."

Gerald was only ten minutes away.

With another report filed and Gerald scratching his head about the whole situation, Gerald said, "I suggest you put cameras up to see who's breaking in here."

"That's a great idea, my friend," Jessie said, patting Gerald on the back.

"You changed the door locks, and they come in the window. There's obviously something here they want." Gerald said. Again, he scratched his head. "You know, it's rumored that your Aunt was so rich, she hid money and jewelry someplace in the house, but we also knew—

ma'am, no disrespect intended, but—your Aunt Pauline was, you know, different. So, most people figured it was all just rumor."

"I didn't know her, so I couldn't tell you if it's true or not. But I can tell you I've seen no hidden treasure since I moved in."

"There will always be people who'll believe the rumors. So, I wouldn't waste any time in getting those cameras up and running," Gerald said.

Jessie shook Gerald's hand and walked him out. I went to the bedroom to put the bed back in place and examine the floor.

"I think it's best we sleep together in the bed tonight," Jessie said, walking in the room.

I smiled. "I thought you'd never ask."

"Don't go getting any ideas, City Girl, because I'm not that kind of guy."

I put on a pouty face for a second and then grinned.

"To be honest, I want you so bad it hurts, but you're still a married woman. I won't disrespect you or me, ever, got that?"

I touched the side of his face. "I'm okay with that. All I want right now is just to be near you."

"That's my girl."

We spent hours on the couch, talking and holding each other. Before the evening ended, we discussed the plans for the next couple of days.

Fixing the house was put on the back burner until we bought cameras and installed them as soon as possible, then we would examine my room with a fine-toothed comb even if we had to tear it apart.

"Mais, I tell you one thing, Cher, we will get to the bottom of this." Jessie's exaggerated Cajun accent made me giggle. He put his hand on mine, and his expression grew serious. "I promise."

CHAPTER 12

The next morning, we woke up wrapped around each other. I was happy, safe, and content in Jessie's arms, so I refused to move, even to massage the cramp in my neck.

With a sweet kiss on my forehead, Jessie slid out of the covers to go make coffee, leaving me yearning for his warm presence.

I hung my feet off the edge of the bed. Dressing casual was growing on me. My stretch yoga pants and tee shirt weren't my normal attire for sleeping, but I'd dressed with Jessie's comfort in mind, considering we weren't planning to be physical with each other.

Before I had time to change clothes and wash my face, there was a knock. I hurried to the door and opened it.

"Brian, what brings you out this time of morning?" I asked as I pulled my hair across my shoulders to comb my fingers through it. His habit of dropping by unannounced was quite annoying.

"I was just checking in on you to see if everything was okay."

"Oh, sure. Come in?" I said, opening the door wider.

As he came in, he put his keys on the side table beside mine and entered the living room.

I straightened the pillows on the couch and pulled my tee shirt down, trying to look presentable for the unexpected company.

Brian glanced around the room, then looked at me from top to bottom. "Did I come at a bad time?" he asked.

"No, just straightening up some."

"I see you've been doing work on this old house."

"Yes, it's a work in progress. Like you said, it would look nice with a fresh coat of paint."

"Yes, I did, didn't I? Who'd you get to help?"

I hesitated. Brian was getting a bit nosey, and it was none of his business.

Jessie came out of the kitchen about that time and saved me from having to answer. "I'm doing the work around here." Jessie set two cups of coffee on the side table and extended his hand. "I'm Jessie Leblanc."

I wasn't sure what Brian was going to say. He turned two shades whiter than his normal pale and seemed embarrassed by Jessie walking in the room barefoot, coffee in hand.

Brian cleared his throat. "I'm Sarah's, ah, and her

Aunt Pauline's attorney. I, uh, was just checking on Sarah to see if she needed anything."

"I'm fine, Brian, and as you can see, I have help," I said, interrupting the stare Brian was giving Jessie.

"Yes, I see that now." Brian gave us a look of disgust as he turned and started to leave. "Like I said, just checking in on you," Brian mumbled, waving his hand, and grabbing his keys as he rushed out the front door.

Jessie made a crooked face. "Do you think he was caught unaware?"

We laughed.

"He seemed shocked." I snorted.

Jessie looked amused at my sound. He grabbed my hand and twirled me like a ballerina, then led me to the couch where he handed me some fresh-brewed coffee.

We sat, drinking our coffee, each of us looking like evil twins and giggling between sips.

"Did you see that guy's face when I walked in the room?" Jessie chuckled, taking another sip. "Miss Scarlet, I believe you had you a gentleman caller." My face burned with embarrassment. "I think I have my work cut out for me," Jessie said in a low tone.

"Don't be silly. I have no desire to have a gentleman caller."

"Well, excuse me," Jessie replied while standing as if he would leave.

I grabbed his wrist and tugged him towards me, almost spilling my coffee. Jessie took my cup, set it on the table, and covered my body with his. Wrapping his arm around my waist to pull me closer, he boldly kissed me, parting my lips with his tongue. My body shook, sending my desires through the roof. The taste of coffee on his lips and his warm hands made me shiver. He smelled as fresh as a summer day.

I wanted him so bad. My body arched towards him. I moved my hands under his tee shirt and caressed his waist, up his back, to his shoulders where I drew him even closer.

Jessie rained kisses on my face and down my neck to my shoulder, where he eased my shirt down, exposing my soft creamy skin all the way to the top of my breast. A yearning deep inside had my breath coming in short bursts of desire to match his. His teeth nibbled, sending a chill down to my toes and leaving goosebumps as he progressed towards my mounds. His kisses grew more intense as his hands caressed my ribs beneath my breast.

I groaned with pleasure while my mind yelled, "Please, end this hunger in me."

As he kissed up my neck, his hands moved under my hips. My breath caught in my throat as he pulled me closer, pressing his manhood against me.

"My God, Sarah, I want you so bad." He moaned and retraced his path to my lips. After pulling my shirt back around my shoulders, he rose from the couch, leaving me with an empty hole in the pit of my stomach.

He stood there, looking at me with longing in his face.

I was breathless and so turned on I couldn't speak. My gaze went to his manhood. There was no doubt he wanted me as much as I wanted him.

"We have work to do, Sweet Lips." Jessie reached down to pull me to my feet.

I grabbed my cup, desperate for one last sip. I needed to break the spell of our close encounter and give myself time to come down from the mountain of desire that flowed through my veins.

Jessie and I decided to dress and go check on getting some cameras. When we reached the side table by the door, my hand stopped midair when I realized my keys were missing. I looked on the floor, then started rummaging through my purse.

"What's wrong?" Jessie asked with a worried look on his face.

"My keys, they're not here."

"Are you sure you put them there?"

"Of course, I'm sure; I always leave my keys and purse on the side table."

It was like déjà vu when I'd found my purse in the kitchen.

At that moment, I heard a door slam outside. I peeked out the curtain.

"What does he want?" I grumbled.

"Who is it?"

"Brian." I opened the door before he could knock, his fist inches from my face.

"Sorry to disturb you, but I accidentally picked these up when I left." Brian handed me the keys. "I don't know how I did that. I'm so sorry."

"No problem, Brian. We were just looking for them."

I handed the keys to Jessie and picked up my purse as

we slid out the door together. It was awkward, the three of us going down the steps at the same time, each of us with our own agenda for the day.

Jessie opened the car door for me, walked around to the driver's side, and slipped in. He then stared in the rearview mirror and started the engine while we waited for Brian to leave. At the same time, Brian seemed to be watching us as he left.

"I swear Sarah, that guy is fuming under the collar. I don't know why unless he's jealous of me being here." He paused. "I'm a pretty good judge of character, and I have to tell you, I just don't trust him."

"I don't trust him either, Jessie." I was so relieved someone else got a bad vibe about Brian like I did.

"Okay, well, we both agree on that issue." Jessie winked at me.

"So, where are we headed first?" I asked with a smile.

"Well, I thought the first thing we should do is get some advice about security cameras. I don't know a lot about them, but I have a friend in town who's a genius, and he can help me out."

Jessie seemed to know every back road in Marksville, and before I knew it, we were sitting on the corner facing the courthouse.

"This is it," Jessie said, looking past me at an old, brick building on the corner.

The front was tinted glass, showing our reflection. My heart skipped a beat as I noticed that we looked like a couple deeply in love. I smiled as we stepped up onto the walkway from the street. Upon entering through the front door, we both hesitated for our eyes to adjust to the dimmer light, and then walked up to the front desk. A pretty, young girl with dark hair and huge Betty Davis eyes greeted us.

I stood back as Jessie asked for his friend.

"Steve, you got a customer," the young girl yelled over her shoulder.

From a side door, a tall, young man with light brown hair entered. He gave a genuine wide smile as soon as he saw Jessie.

"Jessie, long time no see. What brings you to town?" Steve asked as he extended his hand to Jessie.

I walked to the glass front and looked out the window while they discussed computers and nerd stuff.

The town was so small compared to where I grew up, but it had the classic small-town charm. The court-house was as active as a beehive, and there wasn't an empty parking space to be found anywhere around the square.

When I glanced back at Jessie, he and Steve were watching me. Before I could comment, another guy entered from the side door. The new guy who Steve called Ned, was tall and husky with dark hair. His gentle smile and kind eyes made me think of a big teddy bear I had when I was young. By the way, everyone talked, I could tell that Jessie was a part of this circle of friends.

Steve and Ned were deep in a discussion when I returned to Jessie's side.

"This isn't exactly what we do here, but I can sure

hook you up," Steve said with a smile of true friendship. "I'll let you know what I find."

After we said our goodbyes, Jessie grabbed my hand, and we walked outside.

"It's good to have friends. Steve, Ned, and the young girl fix computers." He nodded at the office.

"Really? The young girl, too? She looks more like a model or something."

"That young girl is Ned's baby sister, and her name is Shelly. Don't let her looks fool you. She can hang with the big guys." Jessie chuckled.

"What's so funny?" I asked.

"Shelly rolls her eyes whenever she sees me and tries hard to ignore me because I called her a snob in school. She's never forgiven me. She acts like she hates my guts, but I know better." He shrugged like it didn't bother him the least bit. "Anyhow, they're all freaking awesome when it comes to computers. Steve has cameras up at his house, so I knew he'd be the person to ask. Not to mention, the guy is a whiz at everything he puts his mind to. Since we go way back, he's willing to help us out. This is part of why I decided to give up the city life for home." Jessie squeezed my hand. "I could have stayed in the corporate world after college, but it wasn't home. It just didn't feel real." Jessie paused. "Sarah, this is real." He pulled my hand to his heart. "The true bonding with people is real."

At that moment, I understood what he'd meant when he'd whispered on the steps of his house.

"Where there is love, miracles happen."

For the first time, I realized the world I came from was just glitter and glitz, and nothing real. My marriage was fake. My friends were fake. My church was fake. I had nothing real in New York. At the time, I'd replaced the love of my parents with what seemed real because it made me feel important, set apart, and admired. Nevertheless, in all reality, it was just a way to feel good about myself in an artificial world.

How could I have been so stupid? There was no love anywhere in my life, and there sure weren't any miracles.

A terrible emptiness filled my heart, and tears ran down my cheeks as we drove away.

"Why are you crying, Boo? Did I say something wrong?"

"No, Jessie." I touched his arm. "You said everything right."

CHAPTER 13

*J*essie pulled into a parking lot next to a Taco Bell, cut off the engine of the car, and turned to face me.

"We're not going anywhere until you tell me why you're crying." Jessie's face was full of concern.

With tears streaming down my face, I confided in Jessie. "I have nothing real in my life. My entire world is just one big episode out of a soap opera."

Jessie took the cap off his head and combed his dark shiny hair back with his fingers.

I wondered if that gesture was a sign of him not knowing what to say, or some kind of stalling tactic until he knew what to do next.

"Sarah, I'm not sure I understand."

"You whispered in my ear yesterday that 'Where there is love, there are miracles.'" I cocked my head to look in Jessie's eyes. "I didn't understand the true meaning of what you said until right now." My heart raced so hard I was afraid it would burst out of my chest. The ache was so strong I could hardly talk. "I've struggled so hard to be somebody people would admire and want to emulate. My desire was to accumulate money, stature, a husband of high standing, and a church where only the elite went." My heart exploded with a desire to get my past off my chest. My mouth ran away with me, and my burden lightened.

"But none of it was real. I just now realized, for the past several years, my life in New York has been a lie. I lead an artificial life with artificial people trying to fit into a mold I thought was right. Nothing was genuine. My life was nothing like what you have." Jessie fumbled in the car door to hand me a rumpled used napkin with ketchup on it. My heart melted with such a genuine gesture. "My marriage, my so call friends, my church, my BMW, none of it was real. It was all about money. I'm not even sure I even know who God is. If God isn't all about money, then who is he?"

I paused and took a deep breath, hoping to gain a measure of control over my rampant emotions. "However, when I lost everything, there was no one there for me. That miracle you talked about? I saw it today in the eyes of your friends. They really care. They have your back." Jessie reached over to wipe a tear that was running to my chin. "I feel like I was living in a paper doll world where nothing was real. There was no love in anything I said or did," I said, sighing in guilt. "When I lost everything in New York, the light went out in my soul, and I found I had no love to turn to. Do you understand?" I asked, not really wanting a response. I stared off into space, realizing how shallow of a person I had become.

"I, uh, uh," Jessie stuttered and placed his warm hand on my shoulder.

"No one had my back. No one," I said, blowing my nose. "It was like I was seeing my life through rose-colored glasses. If it wasn't for the angels who appeared to me, I would still be lost in New York in that artificial world I created."

"Whoa, did you say angels?" Jessie gasped.

I searched under the seat for more tissues as I told Jessie of my encounters in the condo.

"You may not know God, but He sure knows you. Just because the life you led before wasn't real, doesn't mean you haven't found real here. Sarah, I'm as real as they come. My feelings for you are from the heart. They're real. Don't be sad." Jessie combed his fingers through my hair. "Be happy. Yell from the top of your lungs, because God has shown you a way out of the artificial world you were in, into a new real world with love and light and the possibilities of miracles around every corner," Jessie said with enthusiasm. "Promise me you won't let your past dictate your future."

My heart expanded. "You're right, Jessie. I should be happy. I've been thinking of this all wrong. I was kicked to the curb with nothing. I lost everything, then I came to this dreadful house, in the middle of a state I never would have visited, much less lived in, where there's been one disaster after another. All I've wanted was to go back to my comfortable condo. Living in this, this nature has been pure torture. The woods and I aren't friends."

Wiping my nose, I stared out the window so I wouldn't see Jessie's reaction. "There's a beauty here I've never seen before, and best of all, it feels real." Jessie's fingers tipped my chin towards him. "I've looked down my nose at everything here, feeling it's all beneath me. Yet, the people have been so friendly. Ronald at the hotel, and Mary at the hardware store, and your friends, but most of all, you. Now I know what real, really is," I said, hoping in my heart I hadn't disappointed him.

Jessie gazed at me strangely. His mouth parted as if he couldn't believe what I'd said. His reaction changed as I searched his face, and he laughed. "That's my girl. You stick with old Jessie here, and I'll show you real."

I giggled at his raised eyebrow and the twinkle in his eyes. I knew there were many layers to the real he was talking about. My heart was lighter after our conversation. Being honest with Jessie about my feelings felt right. I could never tell Hank anything. It was always about him.

I wondered if he knew yet that I was gone. Could he track me down here? Surely, I had to give him my address so he could serve me with divorce papers. Would he fight me for the house? At least it was in my name. If only there was no community property law. The condo was in his name, and the house was in mine, and that was the way it should stay.

Jessie gave me a half grin, and a raised eyebrow. "Did you say you had a BMW?"

I laughed. "Yes, I did."

"I thought so." Jessie winked at me then joined me in laughter.

Everything was out in the air, and it felt good to know he didn't think any less of me.

∼

*A*s we drove up to the house, the partial paint job made it look so funny.

Jessie glanced at me. "Are you thinking what I'm thinking?"

I laughed. "I doubt it, but go ahead. What are you thinking?"

"I know we need to get busy fixing up your house, but I was wondering if I could tear your room apart?" Jessie reached for my hand. "Until we get the cameras in place, I really want to see why you seem to have so much going on in your room."

"That's a great idea. Maybe we can find out what the intruder is looking for."

"All right, then, let's get down to business."

We ran for the door. Jessie unlocked it, and we raced to my room.

"I win," I said, laughing. Catching my breath, I asked, "Where do we start?"

"Let's take everything out of your closet."

I dreaded going through Aunt Pauline's stuff, but I

knew we had to do it. I darted to the kitchen to get garbage bags and hurried back.

Jessie had already taken all the shoes out. In case something was hidden inside, I checked each pair, then tossed them into the trash. Since I was the same size as Aunt Pauline, I kept a couple of pairs.

Next were the hanging clothes. Everything smelled old and damp. I threw everything but one jacket, a couple of pairs of pants, and some tee shirts.

The top shelf was the worst. There were so many knick-knacks, pictures, boxes of paperwork, and gobs of yarn. Everything was so disorganized compared to the other rooms.

"Jessie, I believe someone's gone through this already. I didn't know Aunt Pauline, but compared to the rest of the house, she would never just throw things in her closet in such a manner."

"I believe you're right."

Once everything was out, Jessie started knocking on walls and floors, and pushing and pulling on everything to see if she had a hidden compartment. When his search turned up nothing, we hauled the garbage to the front porch, came back, and sat on the floor.

After several minutes of staring at the closet, I got up and shoved my bed to the same spot it had been moved to several times, then crawled around and inspected every inch of the floor.

"What are you doing?" Jessie asked.

"There has to be a reason my bed's always moved. I was thinking there might be a trapdoor. Help me look."

Jessie and I slide the bed over even further. We were both on our hands and knees, poking the cracks and thumping the boards.

"I don't see anything, do you?" I started eyeing the walls. "Jessie, it's funny that all the walls in here are wallpapered except this one." I pointed.

"You're right. I never thought of that!" Jessie got up and passed his hand over the boards. "This is some of the best wood. Cypress will last forever. It's hard and sturdy." He knocked and shoved the wall, making his way closer to my bed. All of a sudden, he turned to me with his eyes widened in surprise. "I felt something."

"You felt something?" I questioned, jumping to my feet to stand by him.

"Look at how the wall moves some in this spot."

I was so excited. Finally, maybe we could solve the mystery of the moving bed.

Jessie kicked the baseboards. Moving his hand from right to left, he pressed on the wall. At one section, the wall gave a little, and we heard a click.

"Holy shit!" When Jessie moved his hand away, a hidden door cracked an inch. He pulled the panel until we could see a small space big enough for a person to fit.

As Jessie ran out of the bedroom, I peeked inside. It was so dark it was hard to tell what was in there. Jessie returned with a flashlight and entered the narrow corridor, his shoulders scraping the sides. I followed close behind, trying not to touch the dusty wooden slats. After several steps, he found a ladder leading to the second floor.

Being so close to dirt and grime made me nauseous. I raised my shirt to cover my nose and mouth so I didn't inhale any filth. When I got to the ladder, I hesitated. I checked my pocket for anything I could use so I wouldn't have to touch anything and found several old napkins from my earlier crying spree. The thin paper wasn't much, but it was all I had, so I wrapped it around the rungs and climbed behind him.

"You know we need to work on this dirt thing you have going on." He laughed.

"That's not funny. Don't talk to me. I don't want to inhale any of this dust."

When I got to the top, Jessie extended his hand and pulled me up the rest of the way. We were in a tiny dark room. A small desk and chair were on the right side, and the left side was a wall of small lockers large enough for maybe a purse and shoes.

From what I could see, it looked like most of them were already open. It reminded me of a bank vault with cubicles for important items.

"I wonder why Aunt Pauline would need all these lockers?"

The beam from Jessie's flashlight hit the desk, highlighting some tools.

"So, now we know. Someone obviously believes the rumor that there's something of value in this house." Jessie inspected the small open cubicles and found ten that had not been broken into yet. "Sarah, we need to set a trap."

"You're damn right we need to set a trap. Can you

believe this? Someone has the nerve to break into my house and search for treasure. This pisses me off."

Jessie turned his head towards me. "This is the second time I've seen you mad."

"Second?" I wondered.

"Yeah, the first time was when you were trying to get in the pirogue, and you fell half in and half out the bayou." Jessie chuckled. "You were screaming and hollering."

"You saw that?" I asked embarrassed.

"I got my binoculars out when I saw a movement at Miss Pauline's house. That's why I was waiting for you at my dock. That was the funniest thing I'd seen all year. That's how I knew you were a city girl. No country girl would have a cow over getting dirty."

"Yeah, well, you didn't see that gross green frog jump on my arm."

He laughed so hard his face turned red. "Stop, stop. Yes, I did see. I didn't know why you were jumping around, but I saw the whole thing."

I couldn't help myself. I laughed right along with him.

CHAPTER 14

*A*fter supper, we sat on the couch and strategized our next move. Since we wanted to catch the intruder in the act, and not deter him if he found two people instead of one, we left the bed under the window.

"Well, if someone wants in this house, he'll have to break in since we changed the locks and fixed the windows. And now we know the bed was being moved to gain access to the hidden panel," Jessie pondered.

But what would explain the water puddle in my room or the hallway, or seeing my Aunt Pauline by the closet, for that matter? What did she want? Was she there just to say hi, or was she there to warn me?

We brainstormed about how to hear the intruder when he entered the secret passage and devised a plan to set a trap inside the hidden corridor using fishing line.

"We need to attach something to the line so we can hear the door open. Do you have bells or something?"

"Bells? Not that I've ever seen."

"That would solve our problem if you did." Jessie winked.

"I was just wondering, Jessie, what'll we do with him once we catch him? He could have a gun or something."

"Yeah, I didn't think about that." Jessie rubbed his face, causing the blood to surface, giving his tanned skin a reddish hue.

I wondered if he was trying to help himself think better. It seemed rubbing his face or combing his fingers through his hair was some kind of stalling tactic, to give his brain enough time to catch up.

With that thought, I giggled and asked, "Would you like coffee? Maybe it would help you think better."

"That would be great. Thanks." Jessie responded, not noticing my giggles over his physical gestures.

I must be tired, too. I would never hurt Jessie by laughing at him and making him feel bad.

While in the kitchen, I gazed out the window. The sun was setting. I felt bad that we were strategizing, instead of spending it on the dock, watching another sunset and a miracle from Heaven.

When I brought Jessie's coffee to him, he was relaxing on the couch with his feet on the table. I sat in my recliner, admiring him. As he reached to put his cup on the coffee table, he missed, causing the cup to smash on the floor.

"I'm so sorry; I misjudged the corner of the table." Jessie knelt and picked up the pieces.

"That's okay; Aunt Pauline has a cabinet full."

"She does?" Jessie lifted his gaze. "That's it!" He jumped up and ran to the kitchen.

I rushed after him, yelling, "What is it? What's wrong?"

Jessie was grabbing coffee cups from the kitchen cabinet, putting each on a different finger.

"What are you doing?" I asked with my mouth wide open, wondering if he'd lost his mind.

"Look at all these cups. She has big ones, small ones, heavy ones, and lightweight ones. This will work perfectly."

"Excuse me, would you mind explaining?" I demanded.

"We would definitely hear these lightweight cups clanging. These thin ones are perfect. Here!" He shoved the cups at me and walked out, yelling over his shoulder. "Meet me in your bedroom."

I was putting the cups on the bed when Jessie came in with the fishing line. He wasted no time measuring out the line and adding one coffee cup after another, tying them off inches apart.

"I was wondering if we should attach the cups to the ladder, so he'll already be in the secret passageway. Then we can just block his exit and trap him in there."

Jessie stopped what he was doing, came over to me, and tilted my chin. He kissed my lips like a butterfly kissing the morning dew on the flowers.

"You amaze me," Jessie murmured.

"Then we can call Gerald to come to the rescue and

arrest the intruder," I whispered, trying to catch my breath.

Jessie's gentle kisses continued across my cheek and down my neck.

"We— uh," I moaned as he nibbled at my neck. "We wouldn't be in danger that way." I sighed, moving my arms around his body, and dragging him closer.

Jessie leaned down further and lifted me off the floor. Holding me close with his cheek against mine, he moaned. "I think I might have to keep you around city girl."

"I'm not going anywhere." How I felt around Jessie amazed me. I wanted him in my life every day. Hank never made me feel like this.

Jessie lowered me to my feet, holding me at arm's length with his eyes penetrating my soul.

"We really need to get this trap set." Jessie cleared his throat.

Trying to find my composure, I handed him another cup with tiny flower designs.

Once everything was strung, we entered the secret door, and with me holding a flashlight, Jessie squeezed his body into the narrow space and set our trap.

"When the intruder goes to climb the ladder, his foot'll hit the fishing line and make a lot of noise. I'll make sure he can't get out, and you call Gerald. Got it?"

"Yeah, sure." I hesitated. "Only . . ." Even though I was safe with Jessie, I couldn't help but think what if something went wrong? This was too easy. Set a trap, catch a bad guy, and we lived happily ever after? Something just didn't sit right.

"Only what?" Jessie asked, walking out the passageway and closing the secret door behind him.

"Well, we have everything locked up tight. How can we trap him if he can't even get in the house?"

Jessie let out the hardiest laugh I had ever heard, which made me giggle.

"I'm serious." I smiled, trying not to snort.

"You're right. That's an excellent point."

After a moment of thought, Jessie gave me a wink. "Okay, go crack the window by the front door while I take a shower."

When we settled down to sleep, a nagging feeling in the pit of my stomach wouldn't go away. I was afraid that catching the prowler was only the beginning of the problem. The dread was so strong; I didn't think I would ever go to sleep. Then Jessie moved his body next to mine, fitting me like a glove, and my anxiety faded in his safe cocoon.

My last thought as I drifted off was that it was almost midnight, and in Jessie's arms, everything felt right with the world.

CHAPTER 15

The clanging of coffee cups and the bounce from Jessie bounding from the bed startled me out of a deep sleep.

"Hurry! call Gerald. I have him trapped!" Jessie yelled before I could get my bearings.

Mind fuzzy, I fumbled for my phone and dropped it on the bed. I thanked God it didn't hit the floor as I found it in the covers and called Gerald.

"Gerald, it's Sarah Hamilton. Please come fast. We have an intruder trapped in the house." My voice shook so hard, I hoped he understood me.

The intruder's banging and aggressive kicks were constant, but Jessie succeeded in keeping the intruder trapped.

It seemed like forever before Gerald got there with backup, when in reality, he was minutes away, investigating a disturbance at a service station. I was at the front door, turning on the porch light when Gerald and his men arrived.

Fumbling and cussing under my breath about the stupid lock, I managed to open the door with my shaking hands.

"Hurry, Gerald, he's in there," I yelled, pointing to my bedroom.

"Stay here, Sarah." Gerald put his hands on my arms to keep me from following.

Gerald and two officers ran to my room, stalling at the doorway to look inside. When they went inside, I paced up and down the hallway, twisting my hands and listening to what sounded like a struggle.

"Grab him! Don't let him go!" Gerald yelled.

It was over and done before I knew it.

The two officers escorted a man in handcuffs from my room with Gerald and Jessie behind.

"Turn around." Gerald yanked the dark hoodie from the intruder's head, and as the light hit the young man's face, Gerald gasped then yelled, "Billy Joe? What in the hell are you doing here? I can't get a minute of peace with you around. You need to be locked up for good, you hear me?"

"Yes, sir," the offender whispered, his head hanging.

"Take him to the jail; I'll handle him when I get there."

"You know this joker?" Jessie asked with a quirky look of confusion on his face.

"I sure do. He's been in and out of my jail ever since he moved here from North Louisiana. He and his mom moved down here because he was a troublemaker up there in Ruston. His mom thought they'd get a fresh start and hoped Billy Joe would calm down, but as you can see, he's just as much a trouble maker here as he was there." Gerald took the cap from his head and hit it on his leg in frustration. "Listen, you and Jessie come to the office around one tomorrow. It's too late to be messing with paperwork now, and my shift ends in about an hour. I have just enough time to get him back to the jail and settled in before I head home."

"Sounds good," Jessie said, closing the door behind Gerald. He let out a sigh as he locked the front door and closed and locked the window, then he pulled me to him and whispered, "Now that this is over, let's go back to bed."

Go to bed! After all this activity?

The wall clock showed it was a little past three, but I was wired and ready to stay up with a pot of coffee.

We walked back to the bedroom in each other's arms.

"Don't you want to talk about this?" I asked.

"We have tomorrow to talk; all I want now is sleep."

Getting cozy in the bed with Jessie was as natural as putting on my clothes, and I knew my safety was a top priority in his hands.

Being in the comfort of Jessie's arms, I felt relief that we finally caught the intruder and how well our sting operation went. As I laid there going over the events of the evening, I had a feeling there was more to the situation than just catching the young man. Then I heard

Jessie's breathing change, knowing he had drifted off to sleep. I smiled with a feeling of contentment, closed my eyes for the last time, and was asleep almost immediately.

❧

*T*he next morning came in what seemed like seconds. The smell of coffee and someone sitting on the side of my bed woke me. I opened my eyes to see Jessie watching me with a cup of coffee in each hand.

"I didn't want to wake you. You look so peaceful sleeping." Jessie smiled.

I yawned, stretched, and asked, "What time is it?"

"It's nearly ten."

"What? I always sleep so well, knowing you are next to me." I blew on my coffee and took a sip.

"Well, I don't know about you, Sarah, but I feel this isn't over, yet," Jessie mumbled as he readjusted himself on the bed.

"It's funny you said that. I was just thinking that last night."

We spoke at the same time, paused, and spoke at the same time again, just to stop and laugh.

"Okay, you first," Jessie insisted.

"This was too easy. We set a trap and caught the intruder. It feels more involved than that." I yawned again.

"Exactly! It was as if it was handed to us on a silver

platter. What are we missing here? I feel like that young man from North Louisiana was just a decoy. First off, he's just a kid, and he's not from here, so how could he have heard the rumors about this house? There's a mastermind behind this. I just feel it."

As we finished our coffee, there was a knock at the front door.

"Maybe it's Gerald with more news," I whispered as I got up.

"I'll get the door. You put some clothes on." Jessie smiled with a wink.

With my back to the bedroom door, I grabbed some pants off the floor and pulled them on, turning when I felt someone watching me. Jessie wiggled his eyebrows.

"Answer the door you pervert." I laughed.

I heard voices at the door, only it didn't sound like Gerald. As I tugged on one of Aunt Pauline's ugly, flowered tee shirts, the voices moved out further on the porch. I walked barefoot to the door and peeked out.

It was Steve, Jessie's friend from the computer store. They were deep in conversation as they rummaged through a box. Jessie looked up to see me.

"Look, Sarah, our cameras are here already. Steve and I will have this up and running before you know it."

Steve was either shy or just too involved in his task because he barely seemed to notice me.

Neither Jessie nor I mentioned the commotion last night, nor the possible need to return the cameras. Since we were on the same page about there being a possible mastermind, we went ahead with the installation. In no time, the cameras were up and running, and we were receiving easy instructions on how the system worked and where to watch the recordings when needed. With a handshake, Jessie walked Steve out to his car.

I was relieved to know we could see who and what was walking around the property, whether it was a man or armadillo.

Later that day, we were at the Sheriff's Department, filling out a complaint when Gerald walked in and motioned us to follow him to his office.

"I'm not sure where to begin," Gerald said, shaking his head from side to side. He pointed to the two wooden chairs. "Have a seat. Billy Joe's not the brightest crayon in the box, and he's definitely not a leader. He's your common every day hooligan, young, immature, and to be honest, stupid." He took his reading glasses off and threw them on his desk, rubbing his face, just as Jessie did at times. "He's a liar and a shoplifter. He only wants to spend money to buy beer. He's never broken into a house. He doesn't have two brain cells to rub together, and he's too lazy to try. His mom doesn't know what to do with him. When I talked to him last night, I found out that Billy Joe's not working alone."

Jessie and I looked at each other.

"We kind of felt like there was more to this," Jessie said.

"Billy Joe said someone contacted him by phone and offered to give him a lot of money to open some small cubicles behind a hidden wall in your house. He said the man would call him back in a couple of days for an update and to find out where to send his money once the job was done. The bad news is, Billy Joe said he lost his phone somewhere in your house last night during all the commotion. Oh, did I mention, Billy Joe said the man has some kind of accent?"

My mind was full of questions. Who was this man? How did he know of the secret passageway? How did he meet Billy Joe? But the only question that came out was, "What kind of accent does he have?"

"Billy Joe isn't sure. He never gave a name, just that he would call him back later. I think we should drive out to your place and find that phone."

"That's a great idea." I stood, excited to find the underlying cause of the mess.

~

*W*e had just pulled up in the driveway when I got that chill again. Jessie grabbed my arm with a questioning look in his eyes.

"Something's not right," I said.

Jessie and I went up the steps with Gerald right behind us. We entered my bedroom to see the wall open.

"I thought we closed that panel."

"We did." Jessie looked at me with his forehead crinkled.

"Step aside." Gerald walked to the open wall, drew his gun, and turned on his flashlight before going inside the secret passageway.

Jessie followed Gerald while I waited by the opening. After several minutes, they returned.

"Someone's been here, Sarah," Jessie announced.

"Oh no, I knew this wasn't over yet. Did they do anything?"

"Yes. The rest of the boxes have been broken into. They must've found Billy Joe's phone, too, because it's nowhere to be found. I'm sorry, Miss Sarah; I hope they didn't get anything of value," Gerald said.

"Well, if they didn't find anything, you can bet they'll be back," Jessie announced.

"Thanks for the great news." *Like I didn't know that already*. Then it hit me. "Jessie, Jessie, we can look at the recordings!" I exclaimed.

Jessie and I flew down the hall with Gerald fast behind us.

"Recordings?" Gerald asked.

We settled in to watch the front porch recordings. At first, there was nothing, but about halfway through the back door recordings, we saw someone. He had on a black mid-length jacket, black pants, and a black wide-brimmed hat. He never looked up. The intruder fumbled at the backdoor for a minute, then entered. After about twenty or thirty minutes, he came out as he'd gone in, with nothing visibly taken.

"His build reminds me of the guy who was standing at the foot of my bed the other night. You know the one who was moving my bed to the side. He ran out the door before I could get a good look at him. He was short and stocky just like that."

"You're probably right, Sarah. It's probably the same man." Gerald paused. "Since it looks like he left with nothing, you can be sure he'll be back." Gerald stood up and went to the back door to examine it. "Jessie, it doesn't look like it was broken into, but it does look kind of flimsy. You may want to add a deadbolt to this door."

"I just changed the locks, but you're right, Gerald. I should have added a deadbolt, and maybe even a chain."

"With everything that's going on here, the more protection the better," Gerald announced.

"You got it, Gerald. Thanks for all your help."

"Well, that's what I get paid the big bucks for." Gerald winked. He waved at us as he headed to the door. "Don't worry, Miss Sarah. We'll find out what's going on here. It may take a little time, but we'll get him. Call if you need me."

"Sure will, Gerald. I got your number." I smiled.

I couldn't imagine having such good friends as Jessie had in Gerald and Steve, and who knew how many more. In New York, no one would spit on me, even if I was on fire.

As much as I'd missed my job and condo, I couldn't help but be thankful I was right where I was, even with all the problems.

CHAPTER 16

*J*essie checked the clock, and then looked at me. "You want to take a boat ride to my place?"

I grabbed his hand. We ran out the back door and down the stairs. I knew he wanted to watch the sun go down with his parents, and I was looking forward to it, too.

The further from the house we got, further the problems and memories of the last several days were. The peacefulness of the swamp soothed me. The slight breeze on the water uplifted my spirit.

As I settled on the steps at Jessie's house, he moved behind me and held me snug against his chest, watching and waiting for the sun to slide behind the trees.

"There." Jessie pointed to the dock.

Just visible to the naked eye were his parents watching the same sunset. My heart filled with such joy that my eyes watered, and a tear made its way down my cheek. Somehow, somewhere, something gave me the privilege of walking into a hidden chamber in time, where miracles happened, a place known only by a few chosen to experience love, peace, and protection from God Himself.

Jessie tightened his grip as darkness descended around us like a blanket, and his parents disappeared along with the sunset.

After several minutes of enjoying our togetherness, Jessie jumped up and ran inside to gather more clean clothes, and we headed back to my house.

Once we tied off the boat, I turned to Jessie.

"You're so lucky."

"What do you mean?"

"You lead such a slow-paced life, with genuine friends, and most of all you get to see your parents. I wish I could see my parents again. It feels like an eternity since I've seen them."

"Well, just because you don't see them, doesn't mean they're not here," Jessie said.

"Yeah, I guess," I mumbled my response in disappointment.

"Don't be sad, boo. Your life is just starting over in a new location. Give it time, and watch it grow. You'll see, with me in your life, you and I will live in peace and harmony, just the way God intended." Jessie grinned.

"You're right. I have a new beginning with you by my side," I said, reaching to touch his face. "You've shown me more compassion and caring since I've been here, than I have ever known. I know this is mushy talk, but you've made my life meaningful."

"I can't imagine sharing these special moments in my life with anyone else." Jessie bent down to kiss my forehead.

My heart was melting like a stick of butter on a summer day. I couldn't believe how much I depended on him. A part of me didn't want the mystery of the old house to end if it meant that he wouldn't be a part of it. He was such a good-hearted person, the type who would give you his last dollar or the shirt off his back. He flowed with life like the waters of the bayous. I knew there wasn't anything he couldn't or wouldn't do for me.

He said he would cook up something special and insisted I get comfortable as he took over the kitchen.

Was there nothing he couldn't do? Our meal for the evening was a delicious smelling dish called crawfish fettuccini. I didn't understand why he wasn't married or dating someone.

"Oh my God, Jessie who taught you to cook like this?" I asked after my first bite of the delectable dish.

"Mais, it be my grandma-ma and my mom, Cher," Jessie said in the thick Cajun accent he'd hidden so well since I'd met him.

"You sound like everyone else around here." I giggled, my fork inches from my lips.

"Mais, Cher, I be from here, you know."

In New York, there were plenty of delicacies to

choose from in the most expensive restaurants. Fourchu lobster. Beluga caviar. Wagyu Beef. Why eat crawfish when I could choose one of those? Any crustacean known as a mudbug was below me, or so I'd thought. The shallow person I'd become was ignorant because Jessie's simple dish put the city's fancy food to shame.

When my belly was full, and the dishes were soaking, Jessie turned on the old radio sitting on the counter and fiddled with it until he found some unusual music he called Zydeco. Shuffling his feet to the music, he grabbed my hand and swung me in a circle to the middle of the floor.

"Follow my lead. It's easy. Just move to the music." His face split into a breathtaking smile.

His hips shifted side to side in a strange, syncopated rhythm, his feet following a *quick, quick, slow* pattern. I tried to mimic his movements but failed. When I huffed in frustration, he drew me closer, squeezing my hands.

"You're not listening to the music. Now, listen," he insisted.

After a minute of tripping over my own feet, I started to move with the music. Jessie released my right hand and held the fingertips of my left. There was no formula to the steps at all. A joyful, unique sound poured from the radio, and with Jessie twirling me around, the combination had me giggling nonstop. The music lifted my mood and made me want to tap my foot, without realizing it.

When I lifted my head from watching Jessie's feet, I

saw someone in the kitchen doorway. I froze. The blood rushed out of my face, and my laughter died.

Jessie's joyful expression dropped when I recoiled, and he spun around and took a protective stance in front of me, reaching back to shield me from harm.

"Excuse me, I knocked, but no one came to the door. I knew you were home. I heard the music and . . ."

"Hank?" I whispered under my breath.

Turning his head, Jessie scrunched his eyes and quirked a brow. "Hank? Your husband?"

"Yes," I said, clutching Jessie's arm.

Hank strolled into the kitchen as if he owned it. His dark hat, lightweight black jacket, dark tee shirt, and black pants set my mind whirling. Hank had a short, stocky build. Something about his unusual, not-in-a-fancy-suit-and-tie look made the hair on my neck rise. It was familiar, and not because he was my husband.

That's when it clicked. He was the prowler at the foot of my bed that night, the same person we'd seen on the hidden camera who'd broken into the back door. I raised my eyebrow and gritted my teeth because I was certain I recognized his form. I inched even closer to Jessie, afraid of what this lunatic would do.

"How cozy is this? It sure didn't take long for you to get accustomed to the southern swamp people's ways." Hank had such a way of making me feel small and unimportant when he talked down to me in his condescending manner. He was a true salesperson. He could sweet talk you in one breath and cut you wide open in the next.

Being the polite person he was, Jessie stepped forward and extended his hand. "It's nice to meet you. I'm Jessie."

"I know who you are," Hank said, glaring at Jessie's hand as if it was a lump of coal while inching around him to get closer to me. "I'm not going to mince words, because I can't stand being in this god-forsaken country another minute. So, let's get down to business, shall we?" He threw papers on the kitchen table. "I want a divorce. I have all the papers in order. All you need to do is to sign."

I knew in my heart that this would not go well. Hank was money hungry, and I would bet my last dollar those papers gave him everything. He was crazy to think I would sign those, especially since I realized he was the intruder and suspected he was the mastermind behind the break-ins. After almost catching him that night, he must have hired Billy Joe to do his dirty work so he wouldn't get caught.

"You're a sorry piece of shit, Hank. I'm not signing anything." I marched over to Hank and got in his face as Jessie tried to hold me back. Blood rushed to my face, making sweat bead over my eyebrows. My anger made me bold. "You're a two-timing asshole who thinks he can just walk in here and demand I sign something without a lawyer. You're about as dumb as your girl-friend." After not having the nerve for years, standing up to him felt good.

"Good luck getting an honest lawyer around here. This is the most crooked place I've ever been. These people aren't smart enough to light a match." His smirk made my palm itch to slap it off his face. Hank walked over to the kitchen counter and leaned against it, folding his arms. "The way I see it, you left me for this Cajun." Hank gave Jessie a disgusted look, eyeing him from his head to his toes as if he was dirt. "I have every right to ask for what I want. I've got witnesses who will say you left the condo without a second look and moved down here to be with this Cajun, while I was out of town on business." Hank cocked his head towards Jessie. "I even have witnesses who will testify you and this Jessie have been shacking up together. You're screwed, Sarah, and you know it. You sign these papers, and maybe I won't ask for alimony."

"That's funny, Hank, because I have my own witness." I gave a slight grin and thought two could play this game. "I have a witness that you left me for your secretary. Oh, and let's not forget you're behind the break-ins here. I didn't figure that out until I saw you in those clothes, and you're the man who was standing at the foot of my bed. Best of all, I have you on camera."

As Hank walked towards the kitchen door, he turned and said, "The way I see it, is, I gave you a chance to sign these papers, but you had to do things your way. So now you leave me with no alternative. This nice guy just became your worst nightmare." He fumbled in his jacket and pulled a pistol from his pocket, pointing it towards me.

As Hank fired the gun, Jessie jumped in front of me, pushing me backward.

My breath caught in my throat. "Jessie! Oh my God, Jessie," I screamed. I knelt beside Jessie, my pant leg getting soaked in Jessie's blood as it seeped from under him.

Jessie was unresponsive.

I stood up, so furious my body shook. "So, you think you can get away with murder?"

Hank laughed. "I was never here. I'm at a conference in West Virginia. You can ask my secretary. Besides, that little moron Billy Joe was released on bail late this afternoon. He was so furious at you and your boyfriend for having him arrested that he came back here to finish the two of you off."

Hank lurched for me so fast, I didn't have time to react. Grabbing my hair, he dragged me out of the kitchen and down the hall. Pain pulsed in my scalp. When we reached the living room, he stopped.

I was struggling to loosen his grip when his gun fired several times. I jumped and twisted my head to see he'd shot the computer equipment and cameras. What he didn't know was that the Sheriff had already seen the video.

"You will not get away with this." I squirmed under his hand.

"I already have. You could have signed the papers and left me everything, but no, you had to do it the hard way." He released his hold, dropping me to the floor. "With you dead and me still married to you, I get it all anyway."

"Why do you want this old house? You didn't find anything, did you?"

"Just because your crazy aunt didn't hide her money and jewels upstairs doesn't mean it's not someplace else in this house. Only thing is, now with you and your boyfriend out of the way, I can take my sweet time searching for it. The company owes me some vacation. Who knows, maybe I could make this a honeymoon. You know, my little angel's dad has millions. She only works for me to prove to her dad she has it in her to work and not just sponge off the old man." Hank's laugh bordered on hysterical. "Yep, she's worth a lot more than you."

"You're a sorry individual, you know that? I'll tell her what kind of devious, money-hungry fool she's gotten herself involved with."

"That's where you're wrong, Sarah." Hank raised the gun. "You'll never see another sunrise to tell her anything."

I closed my eyes, waiting for the shot. A quick replay of the last several days with Jessie quickly played in my head. The love I'd felt, the care I'd received, and the joy in my heart made me thankful. At least once in my life, I had been loved. It wasn't as long as I would have liked, but it was enough.

Maybe Jessie and I could meet on the dock with his parents each day at sundown and watch the sunset. Hand in hand, we could enjoy the majesty of God's creation. Jessie's phrase came to me. *Where there is love, miracles happen.*

Tears ran down my cheek, and my body shook as I waited for the bullet to penetrate.

"There's no need to cry about it. It'll be over before you know it."

Hank's sarcastic comment couldn't take away the beautiful moment when I realized the angels brought me all this way to find love.

"It's better to have loved and lost than never to have loved at all," I quoted.

"Do you think I loved you?" Hank threw his head back and laughed. "You were just a pawn in a scheme I planned out a long time ago."

"It doesn't matter what I say, you'll shoot me, anyway. I'm just thankful I found love in this "god-forsaken place." I made air quotes and giggled over using his exact words.

Hank lowered the pistol some. "You've really lost your mind, haven't you? I'm about to put you six feet under, and you're laughing about love."

I laughed even harder, leaving Hank with a bewildered look on his face.

Over Hank's shoulder, I saw Jessie ease around the corner. He was pale and bloody, leaning sideways on the wall for support.

"No, I just realized I finally found love. I don't think I really loved you either. I love Jessie."

"Too bad he'll never know it," Hank growled. He raised his arm, but before he could fire, Jessie hit him over the head.

A wild shot rang out, and I heard a loud thud. I lifted

my head to see Jessie standing over Hank with a crowbar in his hand.

"Are you all right?" Jessie asked in a weak, thready voice. He dropped the crowbar and leaned against the wall.

Dazed and shocked, it took me a moment to realize I wasn't hurt. Did his shot miss me?

"Man, that was a close call." Jessie started sliding down the wall, leaving a blood trail. "Call Gerald," Jessie whispered as he lost consciousness.

"Oh my God, Jessie." I started to cry. I tried to scramble to my feet, but my legs were like rubber noodles. Holding on to a side table, then the wall, I made my way to my phone and called Gerald.

Lost in time, I sat next to the man I loved. My heart ached for the man I'd known for such a short time.

There was only one other time in my life I'd felt an empty, agonizing pain in my chest. The loss of my parents had almost killed me. Tears streamed down my face like Niagara Falls. Sometime later, the front door slammed against the wall, and footsteps thundered towards me. I looked up, thankful Gerald and his deputies had arrived.

Gerald knelt by my side while the deputies lifted Hank and tried to handcuff him.

Hank shook his head and blinked several times. "I want to press charges on this guy." His hand trembled as he pointed at Jessie. "He hit me and tried to kill me and my wife. Isn't that right, Sarah?" Though his look said he would kill me if I didn't agree, Hank's voice was begging and pleading for his life.

I peered up at the deputy, and with great pleasure, said, "Book that asshole."

Gerald smiled at me and then yelled at his men. "You heard her. Get that piece of shit out of here."

CHAPTER 17

My heart could rest now, knowing Jessie's surgery was successful. I stayed by his side at the hospital, waiting for him to come to, and pondered how changed my life would be without him. If the events, from the moment I moved until meeting Jessie, had been any different, would I be six feet under right then?

Hank would have really killed me for that old house. He fired that shot at me.

What was I missing? Did Aunt Pauline really have hidden money or buried treasure somewhere in the house? Was it an elaborate rumor, or was it based on an eccentric old lady's ramblings? Was she really a nutcase, or was she smarter than everyone else?

The only treasure I wanted was inches away from me. I smiled as I ran my fingers through his soft hair.

"Excuse me, I don't mean to interrupt." Gerald tilted his head down to hide his smile as he walked across the room and stood next to me. "How's our patient?" Gerald whispered.

"He's drugged to the max right now. They took the bullet out of his shoulder. Their main concern is his blood loss, but the nurse says his vitals are excellent."

"That's great news. I was going to ask you to come in to give a statement, but I can see you're attached at the hip to Jessie." Gerald nodded at my fingers in Jessie's hair.

"If you only knew." Embarrassment crept onto my face like a spider up a wall.

"No, I know, I can see it. You've changed since I first met you." Gerald winked.

"What do you mean? Good or bad?"

"I mean you light up around Jessie. I know a woman in love when I see one."

I giggled. "It's that obvious?"

Gerald nodded. "You know, I see it in him, too."

I turned to study his face. They were friends, probably had been friends for years. If anyone knew if Jessie really loved me, it would be Gerald. My eyes were tingling with tears of joy when Jessie squeezed my hand.

"Jessie," I whispered, leaning closer to him.

His eyes cracked open a bit and his lips parted. "Water, please," Jessie mumbled in a quiet, raspy voice.

Before I could reach for the water, Gerald was up and pouring a fair amount in the typical plastic cup found in hospitals.

"Can I sit you up some?" I asked.

Jessie nodded, and I searched the handrail for the

correct button. As I positioned the bed, Gerald lifted Jessie's head for him to drink. Jessie drank like a man lost in the desert for days.

"How are you feeling, old man?" Gerald asked.

"Who you calling old, you antique, rigor mortis stiff?" Jessie moaned as he repositioned himself.

"Good to see you back to your old self. I was just saying, once you're up and about and feeling up to it, I'd like to see you two in my office."

"Let's go right now." Jessie started to get up and winced, grabbing his shoulder, and crying out in extreme pain.

"Whoa there, cowboy," Gerald said as he helped to get Jessie calmed down and more comfortable. "You're not going anywhere until the doctor gives his okay. Don't worry. That piece of scum isn't going anywhere. He'll have his day in court, I guarantee." An expression of deep concern crossed Gerald's face as he looked at his friend. "I… I've got work to do. I'm out of here." He tapped the edge of his cap.

I wondered why men could not show true emotion with each other. Why did they always have to run away and act so macho?

The afternoon dragged on as we waited for the doctor to make his appearance. It was so late now, I worried he wouldn't come until the next day. After several hours, boredom set in. I was sitting in a chair with my legs extended on Jessie's bed, and Jessie's hand resting on my foot. We were between this world and the land of nod when the doctor walked in with a nurse.

After a quick look at the wound and reading his vital signs, the doctor wrote something in his chart. "If all is well in the morning, you can go home," the doctor mumbled under his breath, never taking his eye off the chart.

I knew Jessie was ready to go home right then, but there was no way I was letting him out of my sight until we got the okay.

"You need to go back to the house and get some rest," Jessie announced.

"No way, I'm not leaving your side. I'll be right here in this chair if you need anything," I said as I tucked the sheets around him and kissed him good night.

Going back to the house without Jessie was not going to happen. It didn't take much for me to talk myself into staying right there. After making sure he was all right, I snuggled into a blanket and made myself as comfortable as possible.

❧

*M*orning came too early for me. Between the hard chair and with the nurses' nightly activities, I felt like I hadn't slept at all. The previous night's events circled round and round in my head like a bad nightmare.

By midmorning, a different doctor came to examine Jessie. When he was finished, he wrote a prescription for painkillers and gave us the okay to leave.

Once release papers were signed, Jessie and I looked

at each other and grinned from ear to ear. It was as if we were young kids finding out school was canceled because of snow.

It was a good feeling to drive up to the house knowing our troubles were behind us and everything would be taken care of. My heart leapt with joy because I didn't have to stay there alone and that Jessie, who I was so in love with, would be with me. The thought of him going home once he was better was too depressing. In the meantime, I would try to come up with reasons to keep him there.

The house seemed welcoming when we walked in. Despite the blood trail from the kitchen to the living room, it felt like it was glad we were home. Maybe it was just me feeling thankful that everyone and everything was all right.

Once Jessie was settled in my old blue recliner, I made gumbo, a Cajun dish he'd requested. "You really can't mess it up, unless..."

"Unless what?" I asked.

"Unless you don't season it enough." Jessie's grin was crooked.

He told me step by step what to do. I ran back and forth to get instructions and offer tastes until I was sure it was edible. When Jessie announced it was perfection, I fixed our bowls and joined him in the living room. After the meal was finished, and the dishes washed, I cleaned up the blood.

It didn't take long for exhaustion to hit us, so we settled into bed. It was good to be in his arms again.

We rehashed the events with Hank and Billy Joe and the possible outcome of court; made plans to visit Gerald for paperwork and then talked about our plans for the house and us. Tears rolled down my cheeks when he told me he didn't want us to be apart, and that he wanted us to be one.

"Once all this legal stuff is over, and things get back to normal, I want to marry you on the dock at my house. It has to be at sunset, so my folks can be there."

"So, are you proposing?" I asked with anticipation and a knot in my throat.

"I guess I'm kind of jumping the gun. I want to marry you more than anything, but I can't ask you right now while we have so many loose ends." Jessie winced as he propped himself up on his good elbow and looked at me. "You're technically still a married woman, Sarah. I wouldn't feel right proposing. Do you know what I mean?"

"I understand, sweetheart," I said, caressing his face. "I guess I need to get a new lawyer. I don't trust that Thibodeaux guy. You know?"

"I know what you mean. Give me a couple of weeks to get back on my feet and ask around, and we'll get you a good lawyer. Deal?"

"Deal," I said with happiness in my heart.

I kissed Jessie, then pulled the covers over his bad shoulder and snuggled up against him.

"I love you, Sarah."

"I love you, too."

CHAPTER 18

*a*fter a week of not overdoing anything, Jessie was biting at the bit to get things done, so with great reluctance, I gave in and told him he could do a few small things around the house.

We went to see Gerald and filed a report on the shooting, which relieved us and gave us hope everything was finished. At least every other day, we watched the sunset at his house, only we sat in the boat because lifting his arm to climb the dock was too painful. The time together was magic.

One morning, Jessie was out back messing with the paint supplies. On my way to help him, I almost slipped and fell in the hallway. I couldn't believe it. There was a puddle like before. Everything had been so quiet, and a wonderful steady routine was underway.

I grabbed a dishtowel from the kitchen, but when I returned, the water was gone. Did I imagine it?

"There has to be an explanation for this," I

announced to the house. On my hands and knees, I felt around the floor, eyeing it from every angle.

A slight breeze blew through the house. It was such a beautiful day that we'd opened the windows and doors to air it out.

My long hair was loosely tied back, but as I bent closer to the floor, it slipped down and covered my face. As I stood and flipped my wild mane back, I noticed a shadow in the doorway.

"The strangest thing just happened," I said, thinking it was Jessie.

"And what would that be?" Brian Thibodaux asked, giving me a peculiar look.

I gasped and rocked back on the heels of my feet. "You scared me."

"I'm sorry, I didn't mean to. So, what's strange?"

"Oh, I, uh, I thought I saw dirt right here, but now I don't see it." Since Brian had teased me about my reactions when I first saw the house, he knew I was a bit OCD when it came to grime, so my story was believable. "So, what brings you here, Brian?" I asked, but my mind was still on the puddle.

"Well, I saw you had some action out here last week, and I came to check on you."

"Oh yeah, that was kind of scary, but it's over and done now. Hank will get what's coming to him."

"Hank? That's your husband, right?"

"Yes, he is." Hank's name started my mind whirling again. *How could I have been so stupid to marry that poor excuse for a man, that leech, that, that vampire? How could I let him drain me dry emotionally, physically, and in more ways than I want to admit? What was wrong with me?*

Brian fiddled with his newly acquired mustache as if he was in deep thought. Something about him was off. He seemed distant. In fact, he looked different, and it wasn't the new facial hair. I studied his appearance and wondered if he was going through some personal problems. His clothes were wrinkled and his face stubbled with several days' growth. Where was that strong cologne he always wore? Not that I was complaining, but his scent normally choked me.

"So, did Hank say anything? Like, why he was here?" Brian asked, interrupting my reflection.

"Not really. Just the old wives' tale about hidden treasure," I replied.

Brian cleared his throat. "Oh. Not to change the subject, but someone approached me the other day, wanting to know if you'd be willing to sell this place."

"Sell it? I just got it."

"Yeah, I know. It's not worth much, but with the money, you could go back to New York and pick up where you left off. You wouldn't have to take care of this old place in the swamps. You know you don't like the swamps and nature."

"Hmm." Everything he said was true, but not near as true as it was when I'd gotten there. The old place was growing on me.

"Well, think about it," Brian said as he walked to the door. "Oh, I almost forgot! I have more papers for you to sign. I'll come back in a day or two with them."

"Okay, sure," I said, wondering how a lawyer could forget important legal matters.

I was extremely eager to get him out of my house. Brian's sickening niceness made my skin crawl and made me think of a wolf in sheep's clothing. Maybe it was all the dealings I'd had with men and women in New York. On the other hand, maybe deep down inside, I knew he was somehow connected to all the crap with Hank, Billy Joe, and the break-ins. I couldn't prove it, but I sure felt it.

Jessie walked in the back door minutes after Brian left out the front.

"What did that joker want?" Jessie said in disgust.

"It seems someone's interested in buying this old house."

"Who?" he asked with a gleam of astonishment in his eyes.

"I didn't ask. Brian seems to think whoever it is would pay enough for me to go back to New York and pick up where I left off."

Jessie eyed me with concern. "You're a country girl, now; you've outgrown that city life." Jessie paused and gave me a hopeful look.

"Of course I've outgrown the city life. You know that." I really wasn't sure I was one hundred percent country girl. There were some experiences I missed, like the weekly massages, pedicures, getting my hair styled, fine dining, and shopping. *Oh my, I still miss the city life.* Knowing how hard Jessie would take that thought, I decided to keep it to myself.

"Don't you wonder why, after the failed attempt to find hidden treasure, someone would come along now and want to buy this old house?" Jessie asked.

"Yeah. It really makes you think there may be some truth to that rumor," I exclaimed with deep concern. "It sure has been the main focus lately. Is it possible there's more to this than meets the eye? Maybe we're looking at this all wrong. Also, maybe we should dive deeper into the history of this house."

"That's a great idea. We can check out the records at the courthouse."

"But first, let's get Hank put away," I smirked.

"So, whatcha been doing this morning?" Jessie asked as he combed his thick hair to the side. Watching him do the same thing time after time never got old.

The way he held me at night and made me feel safe and loved was perfect. Knowing his way around a kitchen was a definite plus. I couldn't believe how much I loved him. It amazed me continuously how there wasn't anything he couldn't do. I felt like the luckiest girl in the world to have met him.

I eyed the hallway closet and then Jessie. Do I tell him? Do I come clean about the water puddles that were there one minute and gone the next? Clearing the air would make me feel better. If I was going to tell him the truth, I wanted to start from the beginning.

"Jessie, I need to talk to you about something. Would you have a seat while I go make coffee?"

Not waiting for his answer, I headed to the kitchen and poured two cups, thinking of how I could tell him about the weird things I'd experienced. When I returned and settled in my recliner, I started my story on how and why I made it to the old house.

Though I'd shared with him before, I recapped my life in New York, my job, my supposed friends, and my inability to find work. Then I reminded him of the condo angels directing me here, and told him about the puddles of water in my room and in the hallway.

"You know, I really don't understand why the condo angels directed me to come here. Did they know I would be in danger? That Hank would try to kill me over some stupid rumor of treasure? Why would they do that? Why didn't they just help me get a job in New York? I was happy and content there."

Jessie put his cup down and grabbed my hand. "You've told me about your life in New York and the angel visits before. Even though I've been curious, I've never pried, but Sarah, everything happens for a reason, good and bad. Look how far you've come since you moved here. Look at the things you've learned about yourself and your life. It may not have happened if your life had stayed the same, but when it changed in such a dramatic way, it was a wake-up call. Honey, you're one of the richest women I know."

"Rich? Me?"

"Sure you are." Jessie leaned closer. "You just said you were happy and content with your life in New York, right?"

"Yeah, so?"

"When God moves on our behalf, He moves with

precision and love. You lost your job, your husband, and your condo because you weren't moving forward in the way you needed to. You looked up to these things as if they were God, you know, like it was your world. All God did was rearrange your life so you could get a better view of what you were putting your trust in. You were never homeless, without money, or alone. God sent an angel to show you the way. You found out about your inheritance, and you found real, true friends." He brushed a strand of hair off my face with a gentle hand. "You also found out about yourself. I've watched you change from a city girl, screaming because she got dirty, to a person who knows the value of her life from the inside, not the outside. Just think of the difference between the artificial world you had, to the inner meaning of life in your new world.

"You also learned you have an aunt who thought enough about you to give you her house. You learned the true nature of Hank and how dangerous he is." He scowled. My heart fell. Was it my fault that I didn't know how perilous Hank was? "Sure it's been a bumpy road for you, but look at what came of it all. You've even experienced things in the supernatural that most people never get to experience. As far as the water puddles, I think your aunt may be trying to tell you something. It's kind of like a clue." Jessie talked as if he was drawing from experience. "The first water puddle was in your room after someone moved your bed, right?"

"Yes," I said, puzzled by his question.

"I think your aunt was warning you about your

intruder. But the water puddles in the hallway is another thing altogether."

"What do you mean?"

Jessie got up and went to the closet. "I know you probably glanced in here before, but I think we must've missed something. Come, let's take everything out of here and examine it more closely."

I nodded, and we began our search for truth.

It took a good hour to get the closet cleaned out. It was full of all kinds of things that should have been thrown away years ago. In the corner, against the wall, was one last piece of clothing.

Aunt Pauline's light blue dress.

I grabbed it, and it almost slipped through my fingers. "My God, it's heavy. What the hell?"

Jessie took it from me. "Damn, you're right. This weighs almost as much as that sixty-pound catfish I caught last year." He laughed and winked at me.

I gasped at the thought that a fish could weigh that much. My lips tightened with unbelief.

"Your Aunt Pauline was a strange bird, let me tell you. She sewed on this dress for a long, long time, and only wore it a couple of times like her birthday and Christmas."

"It must have taken her years to stitch on all those sparkles. No wonder it's so heavy." I couldn't imagine sewing, much less sewing on those elaborate beads. It seemed out of the ordinary to have such a fancy dress among her plain clothes. But then again, every girl liked at least one outfit that made her feel pretty or good about herself. I should know. I used to max out my credit card shopping for top of the line clothes that made me feel good about myself.

We were tickled about the dress and the weird ways of Aunt Pauline.

Jessie spread it out on top my recliner like it was gold, and then returned to the closet. "Get the flashlight, boo."

I smiled because I loved when Jessie called me sweet pet names. It made me feel special.

Jessie tried the flashlight, then hit it a couple of times and tried again. That time, the light beamed into the closet.

"You know, I still see nothing out of the ordinary. It's pretty much your every day cedar closet," Jessie said scratching his head.

"Well, I've never seen a cedar closet. I've seen cedar chests, though," I exclaimed.

"Well, it's the same principle. Cedar helps keep your clothes, or whatever you put in here, fresh. Keeps the moths away, they say. It's normal for older houses." Jessie passed his hand over the wood. "It really is a beautiful wood."

As I watched Jessie knock and push on the walls, it reminded me of him examining my bedroom and finding the secret passage. Wouldn't it be something if we found another secret entranceway?

He stepped back and traced the grain of the wood.

"Sarah, would you please get me a kitchen chair?"

"Sure."

The chair gave him enough height to reach above the shelf. He pulled on a short string attached to a light bulb on the ceiling. Jessie again knocked and pressed on the ceiling and side of the closet.

"I see nothing, Sarah." Jessie stepped down, holding his arm. "You know, as far as the water puddle, it could be because she drowned. It's kind of like a calling card, if that makes sense."

"Yeah, I guess that's it," I mumbled. I couldn't help but think there was more to it than that. Would she haunt everyone who lived in her house? I guessed, as with everything, time would tell all.

With our stomachs growling, we left the clothes and stuff out so I could go through it later. After the wonderful dinner, Jessie insisted on making, we cleaned up and went to bed, talking about the work he wanted to do the next day.

It made me happy to see him so content doing what he loved. I didn't understand the love of manual labor, but as long as Jessie loved it, I figured, whatever floated his boat.

essie's morning routine was to bring me coffee in bed as if I was royalty. He spoiled me, and I enjoyed every minute. Since he'd let me sleep in again, it was already late as we sat in bed, enjoying being together.

With one last gulp and a kiss on my forehead, Jessie was out the door to start his day.

I lay back and stretched my muscles. Going through the junk in the closet made my OCD very happy. Just as Jessie loved working with his hands with wood, paint, and tools, I knew organizing that closet would make my day.

After dressing, I studied myself in the mirror. Despite wearing Aunt Pauline's old clothes, I didn't cringe at the thought of them not being high-priced, designer labels. My hair was combed, but I hadn't put on make-up in over a week. My favorite heels were in the bottom of the closet and had been since I'd nearly gotten them stuck in the wet ground around the house. My nails looked hideous. What little paint on them was chipped and cracked, and I hadn't waxed my eyebrows in forever.

"Just look at yourself, Sarah. You look like ordinary people. Southern ordinary, normal, down-to-earth people."

As I looked at myself, I realized it was okay to look ordinary. I didn't have to put on airs; I didn't have to impress anyone or try to fit in. There was no competition. I could let my hair hang down and wear whatever I wanted.

Maybe those condo angels sent me there to teach me I didn't have to have a lot of money, fine cars, and expensive clothes to be liked.

I was good enough.

Jessie was right. I had learned a lot and had come a long way from my previous life.

I smiled, strolling out of the bedroom with my head held high. "I'm good enough. Sarah Hamilton is good enough."

With my hands on my hips, I stared at all the closet debris spread over the couch, the floor, and my blue recliner. In my head, I argued the need to separate the mess into three piles: keep, trash, and donate. I found garbage bags and tossed the old clothes and stacks of newspapers. My aunt's house was well-organized, but the closet was stuffed to the max with garbage, much like the one in the bedroom.

After what seemed like hours, I had made a small

dent in the huge mess. When I moved a box out of my path, the side split open, sending papers and pictures across the floor. As I gathered the scattered mess, I reached under the coffee table for the last bit and smacked my forehead on the corner, almost knocking myself out. Black dots blurred my vision. I grabbed my head, trying not to cry as my face contracted in pain. After a minute with my eyes shut tight, a tear escaped, but I sucked it up and got back to work, sorting the papers. Anything that looked legal, I put aside to read later, but the old bills went in the garbage.

My final task was sorting the pictures. Aunt Pauline had an amazing assortment of photos of her as a baby, her growing up, and of her, with friends at the local school, she'd attended. I spent hours cross-legged on the floor, getting to know my Aunt by piecing together the snapshots of her life, one at a time, until I felt I'd lived her adventures with her.

What amazed me most was her uncanny resemblance to my mother, long white hair, facial features, and all. Since I was the spitting image of my mom, I wondered if that's what I would look like when I got old.

Her life's tale left me with questions, though. Why didn't Aunt Pauline ever marry or have kids? Why didn't she have much of a life except for this house after she'd finished school?

"I see you've been busy." Jessie grinned as he walked into the living room, finding me up to my elbow in dirt and clutter. He stood there a minute, watching me.

"What are you looking at?"

"If you could see what I see, right now. To think you couldn't get dirty before, and here you are with smudges of dirt on your face, and it looks like you haven't brushed your hair, plus that hair thing-a-ma-jig is about to fall to the floor. Your clothes are dirty, and just look at your hands."

I glanced down. He was right. My hands were black from moving boxes. My knees were full of dirt from scooting around searching through all the crap. I caught a glimpse of myself in the hall mirror and giggled. My hair was a tangled mess. The blue scrunchie was hanging on by a couple of strands. A black smudge ran from my nose to my eye where I must have rubbed my face.

My appearance shocked me. If my New York girls saw me, I'd be the talk of the town. The weirdest thing was, the disheveled look didn't appall me.

"You know what, Jessie?"

"What, sweetheart?"

"Even with all this dirt, I'm good enough."

"You sure are. You're definitely good enough for me." Jessie grabbed me up in his arms and swung me around and around.

"Jessie, be careful of your shoulder," I screeched. "Put me down before I have to take you back to the emergency room."

Jessie gazed deep into my eyes. "What do you say we leave all this junk and do it later?"

"Okay, I guess. So, what do you have in mind?"

"Let's get cleaned up. I'm taking you out."

"Really? Okay."

I was so excited. Not only was I going out with the man I loved, I got to dress up. It felt like forever since I'd worn my good clothes.

After taking a quick shower and dressing in my favorite outfit, I stood in front of the mirror and worried about my choices. My hair was curled and pinned up with elegant ringlets. The slim fitting, black dress with a red belt and matching red high heels was a tad dressy. Was it too much for wherever Jessie was taking me?

I heard a whistle behind me.

"My God, Sarah! You're the most beautiful woman I have ever seen." Jessie walked in the room, grabbed my hand, and twirled me around.

"I was just thinking I'm a little overdressed," I said, eyeing myself in the mirror again.

Jessie stood beside me, and we viewed our reflection. His hair was damp from his shower. He wore a navy blue, tight-fitting tee shirt with skintight, dark blue jeans. His shirt was so tight, the ripples of his muscles were visible, much to my delight. The price tag on his jean's pocket made me smile. He was a stunning man, no matter what he had on.

"A little overdressed? Ah, just a little." Jessie said, a grin quirking his full lips.

"Well, okay then. Get out of here while I find some-thing else to put on. I'll meet you by the car in two minutes." I nudged him to the side and went to the closet.

As quick as possible, I changed into black, fitted slacks, a red button-up blouse, and black slip-on shoes with short heels. Instead of wearing my hair up, I let it cascade down my back.

Jessie was waiting on the porch when I closed and locked the door.

"You look just as beautiful as before." He extended his elbow for me to take as we descended the steps.

"So, where are we going?"

"Not far. I thought a nice dinner and some music would be a good celebration of having all that mess behind us."

"Are you sure you're up to it?" I asked.

"Damn, Sarah, I've been cooped up in the house forever. I've only left once or twice. My shoulder is fine, just fine. See?" Jessie lifted his arm and winced a little. "Well, almost fine."

I laughed.

"What's so funny?"

"You may move your arm *just fine*, but your face says something else."

Jessie let out a sigh. "It hurts a little."

"Yeah, I thought so."

In less than twenty minutes, we pulled up to a small out of the way restaurant in Mansura. The parking lot wasn't crowded, but it was still too early in the day to judge the amount of business they did.

"I'm sorry I can't take you to that fancy place near the courthouse in Marksville. My employer hasn't paid me yet, and this is all I can afford."

My mouth fell open in a gasp as I grabbed his arm. "Oh Jessie, I'm so sorry. There's been so much going on since we met. Let me pay for tonight, please."

"Are you out of your mind, lady? I'm a Cajun gentleman, and when I ask a beautiful young woman out, I pay. I'm just messing with you."

Though flattering, his casual reminder was like a stab to my heart. I really did owe him money for the work he had already done. Where was my mind? How could I be so forgetful? It seemed like since I'd moved there, I had been in another world.

As I looked around at the diner and the people in it, I thought, *I really am in another world.* Compared to the restaurants I frequented in New York, this one resembled my grandmother's kitchen with red and white checkered tablecloths over old wooden tables and matching chairs. Her kitchen was always bright and homey.

He led me to a small table away from a group of people devouring platters of crawfish mixed with potatoes and corn. As I passed the table, a strong spicy fish smell burned my nostrils.

"Come, Cher, let's sit here." Like the gentleman he was, Jessie pulled the chair out for me.

We placed our order for fresh-caught catfish, then sat and watched as people came in the door for dinner.

Before long, a line had formed at the hostess stand. Several kids ran around playing tag, and no one seemed to mind. Waitresses yelled orders, and plates and silverware clanked. It was louder than any place I had ever been.

"I guess this isn't the quiet, romantic kind of place you're used to." Jessie's smile was a little sheepish as our meals arrived.

"You're right. This is more like Saturday night football at a bar."

I was expecting a greasy, heavy meal, but was astounded by the light flaky delight. It melted in my mouth like that salty crackling I once had.

As we were finishing our food, music started playing behind a door near our table.

"Sounds like the band's starting. We need to check it out." Jessie winked, grabbing my hand, and throwing money on the table.

We walked from the well-lit area of the restaurant, to a darker area, where there was standing-room-only by the bar. On the dance floor, several couples were holding each other tight and swaying to slow radio music, while the band set up for the night's performance.

People were still pouring through the door.

"This place is cooking tonight. Since the casino came to town, this place has lost a lot of business. But you always have your regulars who wouldn't step foot anywhere else but here," Jessie explained.

We found a table alongside the dance floor where we

could watch the band without having to see over a bunch of people's heads.

"Can I get you a beer?" Jessie asked.

"Do you think they know how to make a margarita?"

Jessie chuckled. "Just because it looks like they only serve beer, doesn't mean they can't make you a margarita. I'll be right back."

Jessie wasn't gone two minutes when a man stumbled over to my table, a beer sloshing in his hand. Foam dotted his beard, and the bill of his dark baseball cap covered most of his eyes. His dull brown, button-up shirt looked a size or two too small. His belly hung over his faded blue jeans, and his black boots were muddy.

He stared at me long enough to make me feel very uncomfortable.

"Would you like to dance?" The strange man asked, his speech slurred.

"No, thank you. My date will be right back."

The man leaned over, placing a hand on the table. "How about I get you a drink, pretty lady?"

"No, thank you. My date is getting me one," I said louder, gripping my purse and searching for Jessie and the exit.

The man straightened and took a step or two closer, so that his gut was inches from my shoulder.

A fowl, salty sweat and the smell of old beer assaulted my nose.

"Just trying to be friendly," he slurred as he slid behind my chair, rubbing his oversized belly against my back.

I leaned forward, trying not to puke up dinner. The man brushed my side, exposing his hairy belly button, edged his way around my table, and slowly walked away.

It wasn't the first time someone acted like a caveman around me, but this time, I was alone in a strange location.

Jessie showed up with my margarita and sat down. I was shaking as I took the glass.

"Hey, you all right?"

"Yeah, just ran into a predator from the swamps. Don't leave me alone again," I demanded.

As he scanned the area, Jessie moved his chair next to mine and put his arm around my shoulder, showing possession over me. The warmth of his body gave me comfort. My nerves faded away. I sipped my drink as the band began to play.

We sat through several songs. When a slow tune started, Jessie stood and extended his hand to me. Feeling relaxed and safe again, I smiled and took his hand. He led me to the dance floor and held me close as he took tiny steps to the music.

Slow dancing was easy since our bodies meshed perfectly.

His heat penetrated my clothes, and the warm breath on my neck sent goose bumps across my skin. The gentle way he held me lead me to a special place in my heart with no complications, no fear, no worries. Only love.

Everything about Jessie felt right, and I was mesmerized by the magical bubble he lived in. He seemed to be in harmony with the Universe, and I wondered if he and the angels knew each other.

I couldn't believe how blessed I was to have this man in my life.

CHAPTER 20

"*L*ast night was wonderful," I whispered, rousing Jessie as I snuggled closer.

It was usually me that had to be awakened, but this morning I was enjoying Jessie curled up next to me. Relief that the mysteries were finally over flooded me. Nothing could dampen my spirits.

As I put my arms around Jessie, I realized his shirt was damp. I sat up and leaned over him. The redness of his complexion and the sweat beading on his face alarmed me. I touched his forehead, and it felt like he was on fire.

"Oh my God, Jessie! Honey, you're burning up with fever."

I jumped from the bed and threw on some clothes from the floor.

Jessie seemed groggy and weak and was having trouble moving.

"We need to go to the doctor, Jessie." I tried lifting him, but he was too heavy.

When he slumped back on the bed, I noticed blood seeping through his shirt on the shoulder where he had been shot.

I'd thought everything was going well. He was healing. My God, he was outside working again and dancing and lifting me. Oh no, what did I do? I finally found my phone.

"Gerald, this is Sarah. Please come! It's Jessie. He needs a doctor, but I can't move him."

I hurried to unlock and open the front door so Gerald could enter, then ran back to the bedroom. Not knowing what to do to help Jessie was frustrating and frightening. Standing there twisting my hands was no good. I finally thought to get a cool, wet washcloth for his forehead.

When Gerald came in with paramedics, I was at Jessie's side, praying and wiping the sweat from his face and neck.

As the paramedics took his vitals, Gerald walked me out of the room.

"He was doing fine. He even started painting again," I said, worry weighing me down like an elephant.

"I thought the doctor said no excess activity for a month."

"He did, but you know Jessie. He had ants in his pants and wanted to do something. He promised me he wouldn't overdo it."

As the paramedics wheeled Jessie through the house

to the door, we moved out of their way. One of them yelled that they were taking Jessie to the emergency room.

I snatched my purse and keys on my way out of the house.

Gerald caught up to me and grabbed my arm. "No ma'am, I'm driving. Jessie would never forgive me if I let you drive in this condition."

"I'm okay," I said, despite my body trembling.

"You're not okay, Sarah. You're shaking like a leaf."

"Okay, okay, whatever, let's go. I want to be there with Jessie." Worry screamed in my head that it was my fault.

As we followed the ambulance to the emergency room in silence, I prayed for Jessie. Before Gerald stopped the car completely, I was opening the door to get out.

Gerald caught my arm before I fell on the parking lot. "Whoa, there, I don't want both of you in the hospital."

Once the paramedics rolled Jessie through the back door, he was taken straight to a curtained space. Gerald's uniform gained us immediate entrance, and by the time the paramedics moved Jessie onto the hospital bed, a doctor was walking in the room. I was so thankful we didn't have to wait for hours.

Though he kept insisting he was all right, Jessie was weak and pale.

"I'll be the judge of that, young man," the older doctor said as he checked Jessie's vitals.

His blood pressure was a little high, and his temperature was elevated to one hundred and three degrees.

"Now, let's take a look at that shoulder." The doctor removed the bloody bandage. "Did you lift anything heavy?" he asked.

"I don't think so," Jessie said, his voice weak and breathy.

"Seems you've re-injured your wound, and now it's infected."

Gerald leaned over and whispered, "You better keep Jessie from working at the house until the doctor tells you otherwise. Don't make me have to handcuff him to the bed." He winked.

Cheeks burning hotter than lava, I hung my head in total embarrassment. "It's not like that," I murmured.

"I've known Jessie a long time. I know it's not like that. I was just trying to take your mind off this situation." Gerald's grin made me smile.

The doctor left the room but returned seconds later with a young male nurse who hooked up an I.V. with antibiotics, and withdrew blood for testing. The doctor then cleaned the red, swollen area on Jessie's shoulder, replacing his bloody bandages with fresh ones.

Gerald and I went for coffee and settled in the hallway to wait for further instructions.

"Do you think they'll keep him overnight?" I asked.

"My guess is they'll release him once he finishes his I.V. if the blood work comes back okay."

After what seemed like forever, I couldn't take the silence anymore. "So, how's Hank doing in jail?"

"That man has had more visitors than the Walmart down the road." He chuckled.

"Really? He's so far from home, I didn't think he would have anyone to see him."

"He's had several lawyers stop by, and a couple of days ago, a pretty young blonde came. In fact, she's been coming every day since then."

Guess his girlfriend's rich daddy will use his money and influence to get Hank out of this mess. Then something he'd said piqued my curiosity.

"Gerald? I was just wondering. You said Hank has had several lawyers visit, right?"

Gerald nodded.

"Would one of them possibly be Brian Thibodeaux?"

"Yes, how'd you know?"

I shook my head side to side. "I knew he was a lousy, despicable, excuse for a lawyer," I growled under my breath.

"What are you mumbling about?" Gerald asked with his eyebrow cocked up.

"I haven't trusted that guy since day one. He's my lawyer, the one who sent a certified letter informing me I'd inherited Aunt Pauline's house." My memory went into overdrive. Suddenly, everything became perfectly clear. "The same damn lawyer who sent me *two* letters, not one. I remember now. He said I didn't respond to the first letter, so he sent the next one certified. Oh my God, Gerald!" I gasped, clutching the arms of the chair until my knuckles turned white.

"Hank must have seen the first letter and taken it and

read it. How else would he have known about the house? I never told him where I was moving to, thanks to his girlfriend slash secretary. He must have stolen the letter, called Brian, and got info about the house." My brain whirled faster than a tornado, and I blurted everything. "I guess Brian told Hank about the treasure rumors. There's just no other way to explain how Hank knew, right? He wanted the house all to himself. Since he couldn't find anything upstairs in the secret room, he tried to threaten me into signing the house over to him to give him more time to search." My lungs burned for air, so I paused to breathe. "Gerald, I can't prove it, but I think Hank and Brian are in cahoots together."

My mind was on super speed, and the pieces of the puzzle were falling into place.

"Oh my, Billy Joe said he never met the man with the accent. He only heard his voice. Maybe Brian told Hank about Billy Joe, and he hired him to do the dirty work. And, and, and Brian had an extra set of keys! That's how they were getting in the house in the beginning. Think about it!" I paused while my mind grasped the obvious. "Oh my god, Gerald!" I reached for his arm. "Gerald! He, he . . ." I took a deep breath. "He, I mean Brian, came by the day before the last break-in. He took my new keys with him, then later returned them and said he'd taken them by accident. He must've made a copy because we'd already changed the locks; it's the only possible way that Hank got in the back door with such ease. Remember what we saw on the camera? He didn't break in, Gerald. He unlocked it.

The back door wasn't forced open. It all makes sense now!"

Gerald sat up straight and rubbed his face, trying to let what I said sink in long enough to come up with an answer to my accusations.

"If you're right, Sarah, we have to prove it. That way we can lock up that crooked lawyer of yours. He can spend time right next to Hank."

"I wonder what Brian's getting out of all this, and who's the true mastermind. And above all else, what idiot would believe there's a hidden treasure in that old house?" I whispered.

"The story of hidden treasure has been around since I was a little boy. My mom said the first owner was a mysterious, rich, eccentric old man from France or something. Sarah, your house is over one hundred years old," Gerald announced.

I gasped. "I've never asked questions about the house. I was just thankful to have a place to live since I was almost homeless in New York."

"If I remember correctly, once the old man died, there was a fight for the house, and your aunt won. We would really have to do some digging around to get the answers we are looking for."

"Wow, Gerald, the mystery of the old house grows. Would you remember the name of the old man who built it?"

"No, I really can't help you with that. My grandparents would've known. I can ask my mom, and see if she still remembers, but her memory isn't what it used to be.

You know, we can always go to the clerk of court and research."

"That sounds like a great plan, but maybe we need to postpone that until Jessie's feeling better."

"Of course, we can do our investigation later. But in the meantime, I can do some of my own snooping," Gerald said, excitement brewing in his voice.

When we returned to the room, Jessie was in and out of sleep. The doctor came in for one last look at Jessie's I.V. and his temperature. Before he left, he told us the blood work was fine, and we could go once the nurse brought the release papers, prescription, and at-home instructions.

I gave Gerald a slight smile. He was right; Jessie would be going home.

About ten minutes later, the nurse brought Jessie's papers and helped him into a wheelchair.

I was so thankful Gerald had driven. Jessie was weak, and I was sure I couldn't help Jessie in and out the car and into the house the way Gerald could. After getting Jessie in bed, Gerald said his goodbyes.

On his way to the front door, he looked at all the stuff in the living room. "Spring cleaning?"

"Yes, well, kind of," I said, not wanting to get into the whole story of the ghost of Aunt Pauline and the water on the floor. I wasn't sure if Gerald had an open mind about things like that and really didn't want to look like a fool.

Gerald stopped at my recliner and eyed the old,

beaded dress. "What an odd-looking get up for these parts. Just doesn't fit into the swamp scene, you know?"

"Yes, I have to agree, but everyone keeps telling me my aunt was strange."

Gerald laughed. "You're right. Sorry, didn't mean to disrespect your aunt."

"That's ok."

"Listen, I'll pick up Jessie's prescription later and come by and check on him before it gets too late, if that's all right with you."

"That would be great."

As I watched him leave, gratitude that we had such a good friend in Gerald filled me to the brim. He had been our backbone on more than one occasion.

CHAPTER 21

Since he was so weak, keeping Jessie in bed was easy. All he wanted to do was sleep. It was funny because he insisted he was fine, and he was ready to get back to work, but his body didn't cooperate. Hopefully, the next few days would go as smooth.

I spent the rest of the day cooking, cleaning, and making sure Jessie was fed and comfortable. The mess in the living room was a slow process, but all I had was time while I waited for Jessie to regain his strength.

By late afternoon, Gerald brought Jessie's prescription and some over-the-counter iron pills the doctor had recommended.

"So, how's the patient?"

"You mean your friend who thinks nothing's wrong and wants to get back to work?"

"Yeah, that sounds like him." Gerald laughed.

"Come, he's right where you left him."

As we walked in the room, Jessie was sitting on the side of the mattress, trying to stand.

"Whoa there, cowboy," Gerald said, rushing to help him out of the bed.

I smiled as I realized Gerald used that saying in the hospital. It's funny when a person gets a saying stuck in his head and used it often.

"I'm perfectly fine. Ask Sarah? Didn't we go dancing just last night?"

"Don't remind me." I rolled my eyes.

Jessie gave a weak smile. "Yeah, some weirdo hit on Sarah."

"Well, can you blame him? She's a beautiful lady." Gerald said with a wink at me.

The blood rushed to my face. I didn't want the guys to see how bashful I was about the compliment, so I backed up to the doorway.

"I'm going to make coffee. Anyone want some?" I asked, not waiting for a response.

"Does a bear shit in the woods?" Gerald said, giving Jessie a smile and a nod.

I stopped a minute to think about it, which had the guys snickering at me.

"We're down-home Cajuns, Cher. We take the coffee in the morning, at noon, and at bedtime. You know?" Gerald said with a thicker than usual Cajun accent.

As I passed the front door on my way to the kitchen, someone knocked.

"Who the hell is that? It's like Grand Central station around here." I grumbled.

When I opened the door, Brian Thibodeaux was getting ready to knock again. Why didn't he just leave me alone?

"I'm sorry to disturb you, but I have that paperwork I forgot to get you to sign."

"Oh, yeah. Come in. Sorry for the mess. I'm cleaning out the hall closet." I was thankful I had put up the hanging clothes so there was enough room for sitting. "Have a seat." I motioned him toward the couch.

"Can I help you put the rest of these boxes back in the closet?"

"No, I want to go through them and throw away unnecessary paperwork. You know, to lighten the load. You wouldn't believe the stuff I've found in that closet."

"Really?" Brian questioned. "Interesting."

"You have paperwork for me, right?"

"Oh, yeah." Brian pulled a folder from his beat-up briefcase and put it on the coffee table. As he opened the file, he kept making quick glances at the open closet.

"Hold on just a minute." I raised my finger to him, walked to the closet door, and closed it. "I'm getting coffee. Would you like some?" I hoped he didn't realize it was an excuse to shut the door from his prying eyes.

"No, thanks," he said.

As soon as my cup was full, I rushed back, and as soon as I sat down, Brian handed me some papers.

"Just sign here on this page, here on this page, and initial on the last page," Brian said, leaning over me, and pointing at each spot.

Brian offered me a pen from his jacket pocket, and I started to sign the first blank.

"Brian Thibodeaux, what brings you here?" Gerald boldly asked as he entered the room.

Brian stood up, his eyes wide as if he was taken off guard. Surely, he'd seen the police car outside. Why was he acting so surprised?

"I had, ah, a couple of, uh, things for S-Sarah to s-sign," Brian stuttered.

"Sarah will get to that later. Have a seat, Brian." Gerald crossed his arms over his chest and nodded at the couch.

Brian plopped down as if he was being scolded. I was somewhat surprised at the way Gerald took over. His whole personality changed from a good friend to a bad cop in a second.

"Sarah, coffee please," Gerald demanded as if he was my boss.

I knew something was about to happen, so I hurried out of the room and poured two cups before returning to the open door to eavesdrop. I didn't want to miss a thing.

"So, you're handling the estate of Pauline Bordelon?" Gerald's harsh tone made my backbone stiffen. He wasn't wasting any time.

"Ye-es." Brian's voice broke mid-word.

Between adding sugar and cream, I listened a little more to see what I was missing.

"Aren't you a criminal attorney?" Gerald asked.

After a quick stir, I hurried out with Gerald's coffee,

leaving Jessie's on the counter. When I got to the corner of the living room, I adjusted my swift pace to a more normal walk so they wouldn't know I was eager to hear their conversation.

"Yes, but I knew Pauline Bordelon and offered to help her."

"And you're also the lawyer for Hank Hamilton?"

"No, I'm not." Brian squirmed, knocking a pillow to the floor.

"Then what were you doing at the jail? I saw you talking to Hank."

"You know news travels fast. I was there fishing for a client, but he'd already hired some big wig Attorney from New York."

"That's not the first time you talked to Hank, is it?" Gerald asked his narrow eyes daring Brian to lie.

I held my breath, anxious for Brian's answer.

"No, it's not. Hank called me about the letter I'd sent concerning Pauline Bordelon's estate."

I knew it. Hank found me in Louisiana because of Brian.

"After our talk, he came to look at the house several days before Sarah arrived." Brian adjusted the collar of his shirt.

"Is that even legal, showing my house to Hank? And I guess you gave him the keys, too?" I asked, raising my voice. No wonder Hank wasn't in his office, and his secretary avoided my questions. 'Not available' my ass. He really was out of town, looking at my house and conniving with my crooked lawyer.

"He said you'd follow him shortly. Technically, you're married, even if you're shacking up with your carpenter. So yes, I gave him one set of keys," Brian said.

My head felt like it would explode. "You grade, A, moron, you gave him the keys. He almost killed me and Jessie," I yelled at him, dropping the coffee cup, and lunging for Brian's neck. "That sorry asshole will pay for his mistake," I growled.

Gerald jumped towards me and held me in place. Brian cowered, pressing against the back of the couch.

"Calm down, Sarah. Nothing will get solved like this."

Out of the corner of my eye, I saw Brian reach over the coffee table, grab the papers he'd given me, and try to put them in a folder. His hands shook so bad, he missed.

"I'll take that." Gerald grabbed them.

Brian snatched his briefcase off the cushion and stood.

"Hold on a minute, Brian. I have one more question for you," Gerald said, leering at him. "Do you know Billy Joe?"

"Of course, I do. I've gotten him out of jail on several occasions." Brian's gaze flitted around the room. His chest jerked, and his nostrils flared with each harsh inhalation. He tried to escape by squeezing between Gerald and the coffee table.

"Wait, I have one more question," Gerald said as he grabbed Brian's arm and held him in his spot.

Brian glared at Gerald's hand. The instant anger on

his face frightened me. I wondered if there would be a fight between the two.

"I think I've answered enough questions today," Brian grumbled under his breath.

"You can answer them here, or you can answer them at the station." Gerald pressed in close to Brian's face.

I took a couple of steps back, waiting to see who was going to throw the first punch.

"Are you arresting me for something, Sheriff?"

"No, just trying to get to the bottom of the break-ins at this house," Gerald said, releasing Brian's arm.

"I believe you caught your man," Brian declared as he started for the door without a backward glance, slamming it closed behind him.

Flooded with disbelief, I jerked my head towards Gerald. "Why didn't you ask him more questions? What about taking my keys from the side table and making a copy? You could have asked him that. Or demanded an answer about Billy Joe's involvement with Hank. Or, is he the one who told Hank about that stupid treasure rumor? And, and, and I bet it's not even legal to give a tour of my house without me. He's as crooked as a snake, and you know it."

"Okay, Sarah, calm down. Good things come to those who wait. We need to prove he and Hank are behind all this. I know you don't believe it, but it is possible Hank acted alone. Maybe he asked around and found Billy Joe, and maybe it was someone else who told Hank about the treasure."

"What! Are you crazy, Gerald? The writing is on the

wall. He's just as guilty as Hank. He stole my keys. Jessie and I saw him." Frustration? Anger? Helplessness? I wasn't quite sure what I was feeling, but I knew I didn't like it.

"All right, he may be guilty of making a new set of keys from your keys. That's something I can investigate. Technically, he shouldn't have shown Hank the house and given him the keys without you. That's just plain bad business, but so far, we have nothing to arrest him for. Do you understand what I'm saying, Sarah?"

"Yeah, I guess so," I said as I picked up the pieces of the broken cup.

I was so disappointed that nothing came from the questioning. I couldn't blame Gerald. He asked good questions, and he kept me from killing that snake.

"Hey, what's going on in here? Are you trying to wake the dead, and where's my coffee?" Jessie asked as he shuffled into the living room.

"You shouldn't be up," I proclaimed louder than I'd expected.

"I'm okay, but I need to sit down." Gerald and I escorted Jessie to my old blue chair. After a minute, he asked, "So, is someone going to tell me what all the commotion is about?"

Gerald and I looked at each other.

"I'm going to get your coffee while Gerald fills you in," I answered.

By the time I got back to the living room, it was quiet. When I handed Jessie his coffee, he had a weird look on his face.

"I think I might have gone for the kill, too, if I'd been here." Jessie's grin lit up his face. "Wish I could have seen my little city girl jump on Brian." He threw his head back and laughed, causing Gerald and me to smile. Within seconds, the three of us were laughing so hard, we couldn't breathe.

CHAPTER 22

The sun shone in my eyes, causing me to roll onto my back to get away from the brightness. The conversation between Gerald and Brian whirled through my brain on repeat. How many lies had Brian told me? How many half-truths? It was no wonder I didn't trust him.

"What's on your mind, Sarah?" Jessie asked, pressing a sweet kiss on my cheek.

"What if this house isn't mine? Where will I go? What will I do?"

"Sarah, honey, you know I'll never let anything bad happen to you. You'll always have a place with me at my house if it turns out this house isn't yours."

I smiled, but inside, I was afraid. "You don't understand, Jessie. I've always considered myself independent. I've always known what I wanted, but now, without a job, and living somewhere I'm not used to, everything's just knocked my legs right out from under me. If it all turns out to be a lie, then that would make me feel even more insecure."

"It's going to be okay, Sarah. Trust me. Better yet, trust your condo angel."

"Yeah, you're right."

"Hey, speaking of home, let's go by my house this afternoon. I could use some sunset time in my life right now."

"That's a great idea." I totally understood what he meant. Sitting on his dock at sunset was very relaxing and therapeutic.

Getting up and starting the day was the last thing I wanted to do. Lying in Jessie's arms was so comforting, and I didn't have to face anything in life except him.

As we dressed, Jessie moved around a little bit better than the day before.

"You seem to be getting your strength back." I winked.

"Yes, indeed. It's nice to walk around without feeling like I'm going to fall face first on the floor."

As we walked down the hall, I noticed the closet door was cracked an inch or so.

"I thought I closed this yesterday." I opened it fully but saw nothing out of the ordinary.

After making sure Jessie was comfortable in Old Blue, I went to the kitchen to make the morning coffee.

About that time, someone knocked on the front door, and Jessie yelled, "Come in."

Gerald's voice prompted me to pour three cups. I found a pretty tray and used it to carry the coffee to the living room. My smile faded once Jessie and Gerald looked at me like the world was about to end. I didn't like walking into a room to Gloom and Gloomier.

"What's wrong, now?" I drawled. "Is Hank out of jail?"

Gerald threw a folder on the coffee table so hard, it slid across the surface and stopped on the edge.

"Come sit down, Sarah," Gerald insisted, his voice stern as if he was chastising a child.

I put the tray of coffee down and sat next to Gerald on the couch.

"What's wrong?" I asked again.

"I had a friend of mine read these papers. Did *you* read them, Sarah?"

"No, why?"

"There's a clause giving Brian Power of Attorney to sell your house, and he also made himself your beneficiary should something happen to you."

"Did you give him permission to put that in the papers?" Jessie asked.

"Not no, but hell no!" I yelled, my throat tight with anger.

"Didn't anyone ever tell you to read everything before you sign? You've already said you didn't trust him, so why would you even consider signing anything that so-called lawyer put in front of you?"

I hung my head. "I don't know. I know I should know better. I—"

Gerald interrupted. "I took it upon myself to ask my friend, who, by the way, is a trusted lawyer, to investigate the Estate of Pauline Bordelon. That's all right with you, right?"

"Absolutely, yes!" I leaned over and hugged Gerald's neck.

"If Brian filed anything with the Clerk of Court, my friend will find it. Now, on another note, I went to the hardware store closest to your house and found out Brian made a key there, but they weren't sure what day it was. So, I would keep my distance from Brian until I find out if he's even more corrupt than we'd thought."

"No problem," Jessie answered for me.

Gerald sat back and sipped his coffee, but he looked a million miles away. It was so quiet you could hear a pin drop.

"What's on your mind, my friend?" Jessie asked Gerald.

"Well, I have other news." Gerald paused and ran his hands down his face. "Hank's out on bail. I know that was a serious crime, but money talks, and this man seems to have friends in high places."

I gasped as my hand went to my throat. "No, it can't be."

"You can always file for a restraining order against him. My friend can help you with that, too."

"That's a great idea," I said.

"On a better note, I found out through the grapevine that Hank is pleading guilty."

"And what does that mean?" I asked, confused at how that was a better note.

"It means all this mess will be done and over sooner.

He'll do jail time, maybe not as much as you want, but I promise you, he and that crooked lawyer will pay for their dealings in all this." Gerald sighed.

"Sarah, it'll be okay, I promise. Between Gerald and his attorney friend and me, we won't let anything bad happen to you. You know that, right?" Jessie asked.

"Yes, of course, Jessie, but . . ."

"There are no buts about it. Don't forget your heavenly help." Jessie winked.

Gerald's head jerked up, "Heavenly help? What am I missing here?"

Jessie smiled. "That's a story for another day."

"Well, okay then." Gerald slapped his knee. "I need to get back to work. Thanks for the coffee, Sarah."

"You're more than welcome. It's the least I could do after all your help." I walked Gerald to the door and lingered to watch him leave.

"Hey, where's your police car?" I yelled.

"Oh, the car's in the shop. Been there a couple of days, so I'm driving my truck. You know how it is. There's no money in the budget for an extra car to drive."

So, that was why Brian didn't know the sheriff's department was there the day before. I would bet my last dollar he'd never have set foot on my property if he'd known Gerald was at the house.

I waved and went back in, relieved to know I could do something to keep Hank away from me, but most of all, knowing I had friends to help me through all this crap.

⁓

*J*ust as Jessie had requested, by late afternoon we made our way to the dock at his house. He insisted we climb the dock and sit on the steps at his house. Even though I argued about him straining his shoulder, I finally gave in. It wasn't easy, but I managed to help Jessie up the ladder and to the steps in time for another awesome sunset.

Not only were the colors breathtaking, but seeing Jessie's parents left my heart full of love, knowing they did it for him. I felt honored that they allowed me to share that miraculous part of Jessie's life.

By the time the sun set behind the trees, Jessie was looking a little pale.

"Are you okay?" I asked feeling his forehead, wondering if he still had a fever.

"I think I overdid it a little. Would you mind if we spent the night here? I'm not sure I can make it back," Jessie weakly said.

I put on a happy face even though my heart ached to see him struggle so much.

"Sure, my love, as long as we're together, I'm happy."

Jessie's smile was strained as he kissed my forehead.

I got him settled in the house and made a light meal of eggs and hash browns from the food that hadn't gone bad. He'd spent so much time with me he really didn't have a lot of groceries available.

My short time in the swamps had taught me to make do with what was around instead of paying for things I didn't need. Impulse buying just for the hell of it was fast becoming a thing of the past. Making money stretch was never my strong point. If I had it, I'd spent it and wanted more.

Jessie and I were satisfied with the miracle of life, and the life thereafter, thanks to his parents and their dependability to let us know there was more than what we could see.

I'd be lying if I said I wasn't worried about Jessie. It seemed he wasn't bouncing back as fast as the last time we went to the emergency room, but since he was moving slower, maybe he would heal better.

We snuggled on the porch, looking out on the water. The bright moon reflected on the surface, and a slight dip in the temperature kept the mosquitoes away.

My heart and mind seemed to change day by day. The beauty of the city was mild compared to my new love of Louisiana's beauty, and even though I wasn't born or raised there, it was feeling more like home than ever before.

CHAPTER 23

fter a restful sleep, we drank our coffee on the front porch, watching the bayou come alive. Light dew glistened on the grass, and the sun shone down in its awesome splendor. It was hot and humid, but thank God, a whisper of a breeze was present.

The turtles were coming out to worship the sun on fallen trees in the water, and I heard the tiny flutters of a hummingbird who was kissing the sweet nectar of a nearby flowering bush.

It was good to be alive.

Along the bank of the bayou, Jessie pointed out a white bird with a long neck and said it was called an egret. He explained that there was a wide variety of turtles, fish, and birds in the area. The turtles I was giggling about were one of the most common types in the bayou.

"See what looks like a bump in the water there." He pointed, and I followed the line of his finger.

"Yes." I squinted to see the lump in the water.

"That's an alligator." Jessie watched my face waiting for my response.

I gasped, almost spilling my coffee. "You're lying to me," I demanded, hoping he was joking. "Are they always so close?" I asked, grasping my chest in disbelief.

"Well, that's farther than you think. I almost stepped on one sunning next to the dock a while back. Now, that's what I'd call a close encounter." Jessie laughed, holding his shoulder.

"You saw the alligator on land? I, I thought they were water animals." Fear gripped my chest so tight I couldn't breathe. Are you kidding me?

"No kidding, really. Alligators aren't just water animals. They've been in people's yards, or under their house, and they'll even come out the water to eat your pets."

"Oh my god, Jessie! What do we do?" I said in horror. What kind of place is this where animals come out of the swamps to eat you? It was like a nightmare. "How horrible."

Jessie laughed so hard, he winced in pain.

"This is not a laughing matter, Jessie. I'm dead serious." I scolded him.

"I... I know." Jessie wiped a tear from his face. "Sarah, if you could see your face right now."

"I don't care about my face. I don't want to get eaten by an alligator," I yelled.

"Okay, okay. It's rare that an alligator will come out of the water to eat a human, not that it can't happen. Just be cautious. They're more afraid of you than you are of it." He tilted his head towards me and grinned. "Unless they're hungry."

A chill crawled down my spine. "Stop messing with me, Jessie. I doubt they're more afraid of me," I said, scared to think about ever going by the water again.

"For a city girl, I guess you're right. You probably are more afraid of it than it is of you. It's okay, though. They have enough to eat in the swamps than to come bother you."

"Okay, if, if you're sure."

"I wouldn't lie to the woman I love." He patted my hand.

I smiled and leaned in to hug him.

"Are you ready to go back to the house, yet?" I asked. I was feeling a little overwhelmed with the possibility of being eaten by a large, horrible creature.

"Oh sure, playtime's over. We got work to do."

"Excuse me? No, I have work to do. I'll go wash the dishes and clean up some, then we can head back to the house."

Jessie handed me his cup, and I washed the dishes, wiped the tables and counters, and finished up by making the bed.

When I stepped outside, I stopped dead in my tracks. A shirtless Jessie was sitting crossed legged at the end of the dock. Mesmerizing. A view like that deserved appreciation, so I walked closer. His tan skin glistened from sweat. His thick hair was full of soft waves any woman would envy.

"Come, Cher, feel the movement of nature and how everything works in harmony."

I sat beside him, desperately wanting a large brimmed sun-hat and sunglasses, maybe even sunscreen.

"Don't fight it, Sarah. Close your eyes. Hear the birds and the water lapping against the dock. Feel the warm heat of the sun and the slight breeze on your face."

I closed my eyes, exasperated by something so absurd, but tried hearing and feeling the things he was experiencing.

"Feel the peace, Sarah. There are no problems, no mysteries, no ex-husbands or lawyers, just peace."

He was right, at that exact moment in time, there were no problems.

"Now, Sarah, feel the energy of the swamps. Feel it lift your spirit and connect you to all that is."

"I don't feel anything. Only this intense heat and this blinding sun." I sighed, uncomfortable.

"Be patient, Sarah. Listen to nature and feel the energy. Turn off your mind and just enjoy," he whispered.

"I can't it's too hot and miserable out here," I exclaimed as sweat rolled down the side of my face.

"No Sarah, feel past the heat."

After a couple of minutes, I was amazed. I couldn't believe it. He was right. A light mist of energy coursed through my body, like a low vibration of electricity.

"Jessie, I think I feel it." A chill ran down my spine, and the hair on my arms stood straight.

"Now this is church. This is God."

"Oh my, Jessie, I've never felt anything like this before, so subtle, and yet so real. So, this is what I've been missing in my life." In church, I had never experienced anything remotely close. The church was another country club to socialize with others of like mind and standing. "I had no idea that God was so, well, so real. You know, tangible. I mean I knew He was real because I met His angels, but this is so . . ."

"Real?" Jessie asked.

"Yes, real." I giggled.

He turned and looked at me. "Whenever you need a lift from God, or to be in His presence to feel His essence, sit in nature, or sit in a quiet place, think of Him, and just wait. God always comes to those who search for Him. You will feel His love penetrating your body like a cool breeze in fall."

Jessie was a lot deeper person than I'd thought he was. How could someone who lived in the swamps of Louisiana be so sweet, kind, and full of that kind of knowledge?

"When did you first meet God?"

"That's a strange thing to ask me, Sarah."

"Well, I'm curious. I've never met God before," I said, hanging my head. "To me, He was kind of make-believe."

Jessie's expression changed. He looked as if he felt sorry for me.

"Sarah, my sweet, God is love. I think I've always felt Him. I felt the love from my parents. That was God.

When I was a little boy, I would sit alone for hours fishing on this dock, or in the woods, watching the squirrels play, or just enjoying the quiet peacefulness of the swamps, but I never felt alone. I would have long conversations with God. It was almost like having an invisible friend." Jessie lowered his head, and sorrow came over his face.

I reached over and touched his arm. "What's wrong? Am I getting too personal, or something?"

"No, I was remembering how alone I felt when I went off to college. It was so busy and hectic that I lost God in all the humanity of life. It wasn't until I came back that I was reunited with Him. I mean, I knew I wasn't alone, but He just wasn't in my everyday life, like He is here." Jessie turned to me with such pity in his eyes. "Sarah, I can't imagine what it must have been like for you to go your whole life without the peace of God in your heart."

His honesty touched me. That someone would care that much for me was a wonderful feeling.

I shrugged my shoulders. "I guess I didn't know what I was missing. I was so busy in the work-a-day-world of New York that I guess I never realized that maybe God was all I needed all along."

Jessie looked so deeply at me I felt like he was touching my soul. "It took me a long time, but I realized God loves us every second of every day. He loves us in good times and bad. He loves us in the songs of the birds and the sun in your face. I knew without a doubt He loved me when He let me see my parents each night.

Remember what I said. Where there is love, there are miracles. God is that love and that miracle."

Jessie gazed into my eyes with so much emotion, my heart melted right out of my chest.

"Sarah, I will never let you know what it's like not to be loved," Jessie said as he passionately kissed me.

I now understood that where I saw love, I saw God. That was the miracle. Love was everywhere. The love of Jessie's friends, the love from His angels directing my path, the vibration of love from the swamps, the love of Jessie's parents who penetrated time and space to be with him, and most of all, the love of Jessie.

Things seemed to be working out after all. Hank would plead guilty and do time. Brian would eventually get caught in all his wrongdoings. Who knew, maybe one day, I might even find another mystery in the house. *My god, it didn't get any better than this.*

"It doesn't get any better than this," Jessie said, reading my mind. "Since things are moving along smoothly, what do you say, when we get back, we clean the living room? When we finish that, we'll go find that attorney Gerald recommended and get a restraining order on Hank, and most of all, get your divorce started so we can make plans for the future," he said, caressing my face with his hands.

"Oh, Jessie, I would love that more than anything else. I love you."

"I love you, too, boo."

ACKNOWLEDGMENT

Coffee. Yes, coffee. Being from the South, coffee time was always a time of togetherness with family and friends. In my childhood, drinking coffee was always special. I remember sitting together with my grand-mother, aunts, and uncles, drinking coffee, going over the day's events, and acknowledging people during hardships with a prayer in our hearts for them. It was a time of reflection, deep thought, and emotions. Those special times have died off, as each family members goes on to the great unknown, taking that heartfelt ritual with them. Coffee is a memory I will always cherish. Today's grab-and-go coffee is used as a drug to get through our busy, high-paced schedule. I made mention of coffee many times in the book to show deep thought and togetherness of friends.

ABOUT THE AUTHOR

Donna was born and raised in New Orleans, Louisiana. She graduated High School in 1974, and went on to get married, raise a family and travel.   In 1993 she relocated back to Central Louisiana, where she settled with her 3 children, went back to school, and eventually started working for the State of Louisiana. In 2010 her world expanded spiritually to show a new dimension of reality that launched her on a new path, a path of learning, growing and writing. She retired from The Department of Corrections after 22 years and has started her new career as a fiction writer.

ALSO BY DONNA HANKINS

Louisiana Cajun Girl

The wetlands of Louisiana hold many secrets. In this spiritual, paranormal, romance, a young Cajun girl, Marcie, a tomboy raised by her parents on the edge of the swamps, is about to learn some lesson of life from the other side. Several months after the unexpected death of her dad, Marcie starts having ghostly visitations directing her to the middle of Spring Bayou area among the snakes, and alligators to find direction in her life from none other than a recluse that the people of the town called the Swamp Man.

Through many trials and tribulation in the bayous and rivers with her childhood friends, this adventure brings Marcie face-to-face with death. Watch Marcie's struggle with her mind, will, and emotions while she learns lessons from the heart from the Swamp Man and watch her grow and learn the true meaning of life - love.

Web site: https://louisianacajungirl.wordpress.com

Email address: louisianacajungirl1@yahoo.com